Hallowed Be Thy Gore

Gore

Nicholas Gordon

Warning

This is an extreme horror novella. It contains graphic violence and disturbing imagery. Reader discretion is advised.

CONTENTS

Epigraph   VI

1. Chapter 1   1

2. Chapter 2   19

3. Chapter 3   32

4. Chapter 4   44

5. Chapter 5   60

6   Chapter 6   71

7. Chapter 7   81

8. Chapter 8   94

9. Chapter 9   103

10. Chapter 10   116

11. Chapter 11   130

12. Chapter 12   139

Acknowledgements   149

About the author   151

"Their slain also shall be cast out, and their stink shall come up out of their carcases, and the mountains shall be melted with their blood." **Isaiah 34:3**

"Woe unto them that call evil good, and good evil; that put darkness for light, and light for darkness; that put bitter for sweet, and sweet for bitter!" **Isaiah 5:20**

ONE

IF GIVEN THE DECISION between going back inside the church and jumping into a swimming pool full of curdled milk, Mike would have happily asked for a Speedo and swimming goggles. At the very least, the pool of sour milk would have smelled much better than the church.

Mike stood a good twenty feet away from the building—pacing between the cars in the parking lot. Neither the distance nor the harsh odor of his cigarette could cover the abhorrent stench pulsing from the small, rickety building. It came in droves. Mike would almost get a breath of fresh air—a hint of fresh grass, cool breeze, and Pall Malls—but by the time he fully inhaled, the rotten stench of the church would come crashing back into his senses.

Oakwood Baptist had, unfortunately, gone bad. Rotten like a turkey sandwich forgotten in a schoolboy's lunchbox.

Mike supposed it had begun in April when Reverend Joe Mitchell—who had pastored Oakwood Baptist for twenty-four years—had been caught with his hands down the Kimball boy's pants. The pastor molesting a six-year-old was certainly *enough* to cause a church to go bad, but Mike thought they still might have been able to salvage the church at that point. They'd have to cut off the moldy piece—and they did. Reverend Joe Mitchell was thrown in prison, where he committed suicide, but there was no reason to believe that they couldn't bounce back from that, as many churches had done before.

No, the rot had become permanent once the elders had hired his replacement three months ago: a pastor who claimed that God had given him the power to do a miracle. Not *miracles,* but a single miracle. If Mike had been an elder, he would've told that fellow to go stick his miracle where the good Lord split him. But Mike was not, so the elders allowed the man to show this miracle to them.

That was when Tim went to heaven. And that was when the church had gone bad past the point of no return.

Mike glanced back at the church, sucking his lungs full of smoke as he did. It was the same building he'd been worshipping in for the past ten years, but it looked different. The white wood it was built of seemed extra chipped. The creaky porch sagged lower than it used to. The stained-glass windows were murky and covered with grime. Weeds had sprouted all along the trim of the building, strangling the flowers that Doris used to plant. Doris had gone to heaven a few weeks ago.

The steeple, which had once attracted all sorts of pretty birds, remained empty. Mike might've been the only human member of the congregation who detected that the church had gone bad, but the cardinals and robins sure seemed to understand.

The church reminded Mike of a loved one suffering from dementia. Everything remained physically intact, but even though they were the same eyes, nose, and mouth you'd looked at for years, you could tell that something was wrong.

Something had gone bad.

Mike glanced at his watch. 12:17 p.m. He still had a few minutes before the reverend would send someone to heaven. He chucked his cigarette to the pavement and crushed it under his brown loafer. He fumbled another out of his jacket pocket and lit it up.

Mike was a thin, wiry man. His white hair showed no sign of recession even though he had just celebrated his sixty-sixth birthday. He attributed his good health to the rigorous physical activity of working as a mailman he'd enjoyed before retirement, saying it compensated for his chain-smoking and occasional nights spent with a beer bottle.

He turned as a car rumbled into the parking lot, crunching over the gravelly bits of pavement. The little red car parked, and a timid young woman stepped out, her eyes scanning over the church and then landing on Mike.

She tentatively approached him, stopping a few feet away, as if waiting for him to say something. Mike said nothing and found the hood of Lance's car very interesting for a moment.

"Hello," she said.

Mike faced her, unable to completely shirk his manners. "Morning."

She glanced at the church again. Mike saw in her eyes no detection of the rot. She couldn't see that the church had gone bad. She only looked at it with a hopeful curiosity.

"Is this Oakwood Baptist?" she asked.

"It is. I'm afraid you've missed the sermon, though." Mike took another deep breath from his cigarette. Calling the reverend's ramblings "sermons" was generous.

The woman swallowed. "I know ... well, I was ..."

She trailed off. Mike knew why she was here. After three months, the rumors had spread to every corner of the small town. Rarely did a week go by where a straggler didn't come creeping up the steps to the church, poking their head inside, and asking, *"So, is it true?"*

"My father has heart disease and... well, the doctors are just waiting for him to fall over with a heart attack, but... if he doesn't have to go through that pain," the woman said. She clearly wanted Mike to pick up the pieces. Finish her sentence for her.

The reverend had told them to welcome these stragglers. Mike knew exactly what he was supposed to say to her.

Yes, of course! Come right in—you're just in time. See for yourself. Stay a while. Your dad can go first, then hell, maybe you'll be next.

Mike popped the cigarette out of his mouth. He exhaled the smoke, looking over the young woman's hopeful face.

"I'm sorry about your father ... but you oughta to leave right now," he said.

The woman frowned. "What?"

"There's something ... something bad about this place," Mike said.

The woman took a step back, her eyebrows furrowed. Mike couldn't tell if she was listening to what he was saying or if she was just scared of his stern tone. He didn't mind either way as long as she left.

"What's wrong with it?" she asked.

Mike took a deep breath of smoke, letting the nicotine course through his veins. He breathed it out. "I don't know."

The woman frowned at him like he was crazy, but she got back into her car, watching him the whole time, and drove off. Her taillights disappeared down the small, two-lane road she'd driven up on.

"Mike?"

Mike turned to the church and forced a smile on his face. "Yes, Kirsty?"

Kirsty Johnson stood halfway out of the church's double doors, rocking a baby in her arms. She was tall and spindly and had a full head of long blonde hair wrangled into a bun. She was married to Ted, who often fixed Mike's car down at the shop. Ted was a staunch catholic and refused to attend Baptist sermons, even for his wife. So, it was only Toby and Kirsty who came to Sunday services.

Mike thought Ted was lucky to be away from all ... this. He wondered if the man even knew.

Kirsty smiled at Mike.

"It's almost time to begin," she said.

"Oh! I lost track of time." Mike chuckled, dropping his cigarette and snuffing it out. He forced his face to remain neutral as he walked back to the church. The stench grew as he approached, filling his nose with the smell of spoiled eggs, rotting meat, and wet dogs.

Kirsty smiled as he stepped on the porch. It was a smile relegated only to the mouth. Her eyes didn't crinkle. They remained perfectly round, glazed over, staring at Mike, but also beyond him. Mike imagined with an uneasy clarity that if he covered Kirsty's mouth with his hand, it wouldn't look like she was smiling at all.

Kirsty closed her eyes and took a deep breath. "No wonder you lost track of time. It's a beautiful day out." She opened her foggy eyes and directed them at the sky. Mike had never touched a drug a day in his life, and the extent of his inebriation had peaked at getting slightly tipsy on three bottles of beer, but it was his opinion that Kirsty—and the rest of the congregation—had begun to look as if they were perpetually under the influence of drugs.

Mike opened his mouth, so he didn't have to breathe through his nose. Kirsty made no mention of the horrible stench that was making his stomach churn. Nobody did. Mike had tried bringing it up several times in the beginning, but everyone either said it wasn't that bad or wasn't there at all. He'd given up pushing the issue when the new reverend had suggested Mike scrub the church's dumpsters if the odor was bothering him so much.

Mike might've thought he was hallucinating the stench. He'd felt that way about many things the past few months. But Kirsty's son—a four-month-old named Toby—had his tiny nose wrinkled and his wispy eyebrows furrowed as he bounced on his mother's hip.

Mike smiled at the baby and pinched his cheek. Toby was the only child at Oakwood Baptist. Every family who'd had children had left when Reverend Joe Mitchell had been caught. Mike wished Toby could be gone with the rest of them, too. Away from the church.

Kirsty turned and floated back into the church, walking like she was in a dream. Mike followed her, wincing at the stale, stinky air in the sanctuary.

Oakwood Baptist was a direct mirror of every other local Baptist church that could be found in the year of our Lord 1984. Two rows of wooden pews faced a small stage. An organ and piano sat on either side of a chipped pulpit with a carved cross on the front. The organ had broken back in '78, so they relied only on the piano and the choir for Sunday worship.

A large, wooden crucifix—draped with a purple cloth—was mounted to the wall above the baptistery behind the stage. The baptistery was half full of stale water that hadn't been used since the days of Reverend Joe Mitchell. The new reverend said that baptism was an invention of democrats and unnecessary, a proclamation that the church had accepted as fact.

On the right of the stage was a door to the reverend's office. He would be in there right now, giving final counsel to whoever was going to heaven. On the left was the door to the basement.

Mike followed Kirsty and Toby over the red carpet to the door on the left. He stepped ahead of her and opened the door. She thanked him, ducked, and began creeping down the creaky stairs.

Mike followed her into the basement, the din of conversation growing as they descended the steps. The stench was even worse down here, trapped like smog in the room with no windows or doors. Harsh white light beamed down from the recessed troffer lights mounted in the ceiling.

A rough thirty people milled about downstairs. Three months ago, the church boasted closer to forty members, but then the new reverend had begun sending people to heaven, and that cut into the numbers.

Mike waded into the blob of suit coats, ties, and floral dresses. The scent of women's hairspray was almost strong enough to compete with the terrible odor. Nearly every hand clutched a styrofoam cup of coffee. Mike smiled, nodded, and shook hands with everyone. Glossy eyes and lax smiles greeted him as he worked his way to the folding table at the side of the basement where the coffee pot rested.

His eyes flickered to the supply closet at the end of the basement. Looking at the small, shut door made his heart tick a little faster in his chest. His pits grew sweaty. He quickly averted his eyes from the closet and picked up the coffee pot. With trembling hands, he poured himself a half-cup of black coffee.

He sipped it. It was burned and tasted like shit, but he continued drinking. Holding the acrid coffee under his nose kept the stench at bay.

He hated this part of Sundays. He was itching for it to be over. To be back in his recliner watching whatever bullshit he could find on the TV.

The congregation smiled, laughed, chatted, clapped each other on the shoulder, shook hands, and told each other they loved their dresses. Despite their hollow eyes, everyone acted perfectly content. Even happier than they were before the controversy with Reverend Joe Mitchell.

Mike sighed into his coffee. Every Sunday was a constant reminder that he—and Toby, as far as the kid's little infant brain could comprehend—were the only ones who saw that anything was wrong with the church.

All heads turned toward the stairs as Rob waddled down the steps, a huge grin painted under his blank eyes. Rob was shaped like an old teapot—short, stout, and wrinkly. A painfully obvious hairpiece rested on top of his head. Mike had always thought the toupee was at constant risk of falling off, but it had yet to happen so far.

Rob's wife, Vanessa, trailed behind him. She was short, but taller than Rob. Dirty blonde hair hung loosely over her shoulders. The two reached the throng of people and began shaking hands and giving hugs. Rob was the lucky one today. He beamed, laughed, and celebrated with everyone.

It never ceased to confuse Mike the way the congregation treated... *it*. They celebrated like it was the best thing in the world. There was never any mourning or sadness. Only excitement. If Rob had been in a car accident on his drive to church this morning, everyone would've been distraught. But they celebrated now, even though the outcomes were functionally the same: Rob would no longer be with them within the hour.

Suddenly, applause ripped through the church, booming in the basement. Mike followed the congregation's gaze back to the stairs.

Reverend Victor strolled down, his shiny black shoes clicking on each step slowly and methodically. His off-white suit stood out among the off-the-rack sport coats and ill-fitting button-ups slung on the other men. Reverend Victor's three-piece was no hastily made purchase at Sears—it was custom fitted, wrapping around his body flawlessly. Chunky gold rings gleamed off each of his fingers, clinking together softly as he descended. A gold watch caught the light as he adjusted his sleeve.

Brown, boyish hair was combed over his wrinkled forehead. A pair of pristine veneers shined beneath his big smile. His eyes, two beady black dots above his grin, contained more life than anyone else in the basement.

The congregation surged toward the stairs like Elvis Presley himself had just entered the building. Women blushed like schoolgirls. Men stepped forward with extended hands and compliments.

"Great sermon today, Reverend."

"Loved the sermon, Reverend."

"The sermon really spoke to me, Reverend."

Reverend Victor basked in the attention—somehow grasping every hand that reached out to him, thanking each person for every compliment, and looking into all the eyes that tried to meet his. It didn't matter that not even an hour ago, the church had been listening to Reverend Victor preach. They still clamored for him like starved dogs.

Reverend Victor worked his way to the opposite end of the basement—moving as slowly as a celebrity moving from a hotel to their limousine. All that was needed to complete the scene was the reverend signing headshots of himself. The congregation finally gave him distance when he came to a stop in front of the storage closet.

They stood around him in a loose semi-circle, shifting from foot to foot, the excitement palpable. The closet represented the miracle that God and Reverend Victor had blessed them with

Reverend Victor raised his hands. The excited chatter of the crowd flickered out. Silence filled the basement, broken only by the hiss of the coffee pot and the buzz of the lights.

"Second Kings 2:11," the reverend began. Everyone in the church spoke with a regionally appropriate Appalachian twang. Reverend Victor's voice, however, had a slow, smooth, deep south sort of drawl. He had told the church he hailed from Texas. "And it came to pass, as they still went on, and talked, that, behold, there appeared a chariot of fire, and horses of fire, and parted them both asunder; and Elijah went up by a whirlwind into heaven."

Reverend Victor gestured as he boomed these words; his copious amounts of jewelry twinkled from his arms. He repeated this verse every time he sent someone to heaven.

"When it was time for God to call his faithful servant Elijah home to heaven, he did not condemn the man to the earthly pain of death. And like our brother Elijah, brother Rob has been called to heaven."

Thunderous applause ripped through the basement. People patted Rob on the back. A single tear traced down his cheek. Mike took another swig of coffee.

"And like Elijah, Rob has been blessed with the gift of never experiencing death. He will ascend straight to our Lord," Reverend Victor said. More applause. "Now we *love* Rob down here, don't we, folks? It's no surprise our Lord has called him up."

More applause.

"Well, enough hemming and hawing. The Lord wants his servant! Rob! Get up here!" Reverend Victor grinned. Rob waddled up to the reverend, turning to face the crowd. Reverend Victor snaked an arm around Rob's shoulders.

"Rob, any last wisdom to give to us before you ascend?" Reverend Victor said.

Rob's plump face was splotchy. The crispy tips of his toupee jittered as he choked back tears of joy. Mike grew more antsy. He took slow, shuffling steps backward, trying to put as much distance between himself and the closet as possible.

"You folks have been the best church a fella could ask for," Rob squeaked. "I thank God for y'all every day. And I thank Him for Reverend Victor!"

More applause. Mike took another swig of his coffee.

Reverend Victor grabbed Rob by the shoulders. "Rob, by the powers given to me by Christ, I am proud to send you to heaven."

This earned the most thunderous applause yet. Men whooped and hollered, and women screeched as they pounded their palms together. Reverend Victor reached for the gold knob of the closet door and pulled it open. Mike's breath hitched in his throat as the squeak of its hinges rippled around the room.

The closet was small and dingy. A single bulb swayed from the ceiling, illuminating dusty shelves filled with paper towels, choir robes, and old Easter decorations. It looked completely unassuming, but anyone who'd attended a single service at Oakwood Baptist in the past few months knew better.

Rob gave a last kiss to his wife, then allowed Reverend Victor to usher him into the closet. His back pressed firmly against the mounted shelves on the back wall, and his arm knocked over a pack of plastic communion cups as he adjusted.

The reverend swung the door shut. Mike got one final look at Rob's ecstatic face before the door sealed him off.

Mike's back hit the wall opposite the closet. His hands trembled; his coffee sloshed in its cup. The basement plunged into silence. Even the lights and coffee pot seemed to hold their breaths for the moment. Reverend Victor raised his hands and placed them firmly on the door. He lifted them—

BAM! BAM! BAM! BAM! BAM!

The door rattled in its hinges with each impact as Reverend Victor slammed his palms into the wood five times. After the fifth hit, he placed them back where they were and lowered his head. Prayers left his lips, whispered and hurried.

The congregation took their cue and followed his lead. Every head bowed. Hands extended toward the closet. The hiss of whispered prayers filled the room. Mike stood with his back planted firmly against the wall, his eyes wide. The urge to dart up the basement steps and run until the church was two states behind him was overwhelming.

He'd seen this six times before. But it hadn't gotten any easier to witness. He wanted to look away, but he couldn't. His eyes remained open, locked on the door. Watching. Waiting.

Agonizing seconds passed. The sounds of dozens of jumbled prayers multiplied Mike's anxiety. He hoped maybe it wouldn't happen this time. Maybe Reverend Victor would give up, and Rob would trot out of the closet. Then, the church could go back to how it used to—

The lights flickered.

Mike dropped his coffee, but no one paid any attention as it splattered on the carpet. It was lost in the swell of energy that exploded in the room. The whispered prayers burst into full-throated shouts and screams. Men and women began to dance and bounce. The lights flickered again. And again. Snapping on and off with increasing intensity until they were flashing on and off. This egged the congregation on. They raised their arms, praising God under the strobing lights.

Beth, an old, white-haired woman with weak knees, began screeching a rendition of "Go Tell it on the Mountain"—waving her saggy, liver-spotted arms as she belted. Doug began banging his cane into the wood-paneled walls, yelling "PRAISE GAWD!" repeatedly.

Mike wished the wall behind him would open up and suck him through and transport him far away from the revival taking place in front of him. It did him no such favors.

HISSSSSSSSS!

Fog spurted out from the crack between the door and the floor—thick and white. It coasted across the carpet, completely covering the floor within a minute. The stench doubled in Mike's nose as the fog danced around his ankles, concealing his feet. His eyes watered, and he wished he hadn't dropped his coffee so he could bury his nose in it.

The congregation paid no mind to the stench, inhaling greedy breaths through their noses to fund the prayers they screeched and the songs they sang. They danced in the fog, kicking it up in the surrounding air. The lights continued to flash at a nauseating speed.

"Let the Lord hear you, church!" Reverend Victor bellowed, hands still pressed firmly against the closet door as more and more fog gushed through.

The church howled so loud that Mike had to clamp his hands over his ears. Rotten stench ripped nauseous coughs from his throat. Flashing lights made the scene look like some kind of twisted horror movie. The congregation thrashed and writhed; the sea of red faces contorted into praises energetic enough it was a miracle no one's heart gave out.

Just when it got too much. Just when Mike thought the strobing lights would explode. Just when he thought someone would drop dead from a heart attack:

"Oakwood Baptist! God has been here, and he has taken Rob home!" Reverend Victor yelled—his deep, southern voice cutting through the cries of the congregation. He ripped open the closet door, sending it crashing into the wall. The fog inside crested down and out, revealing the dusty shelves. There were the robes, the boxes, and the knocked-over communion cups.

But the portly shape of Rob was nowhere to be seen. The closet was empty.

Rob waited in the closet, trembling with excitement.

The splintery shelves pressed painfully into his pudgy back. He could hear the congregation's prayers on the other side of the door—the Reverend's voice was the loudest. He would miss them all very much. His wife and Reverend Victor he'd miss the most. But the opportunity to go straight to heaven and skip death was far too good to pass up.

His cheeks ached from smiling so much, his tears were all cried out, and his heart hammered as he waited for his glorious reward.

It felt like he stood there forever, long enough that his feet ached, and he kept trying to adjust to stop those damn shelves from digging into his back. After a few moments, he thought he was going to have to sit down and rest until the good Lord came to get him.

Then the orange lightbulb flickered, then went off, plunging Rob into darkness. He heard cheers from the other side and knew the lights had flickered for them, too.

It was beginning.

HISSSS!

Fog crashed in around him. The cool sensation rippled over his skin. The smell provoked a cough, which he stifled as best he could. Nobody mentioned the stench around the church, and it seemed bad manners to acknowledge it at all, since Reverend Victor never mentioned it unless Mike was complaining about it.

The fog built up around him, floating around his knees. He squealed with joy—tensing his body, ready to experience whatever sensations overcame him. How would it feel to go to heaven? Would his body melt away, leaving only his spirit to ascend? Or would his body just change, flesh melding with soul as he morphed into his final, heavenly form?

The cheers, songs, and prayers of the congregation outside grew louder. Rob's heart pounded in his chest. An eager grin welded itself to his face.

Wet.

Something wet and cold slipped over his hands. Chills raced up his arms, but he kept smiling. The first signs of heaven were being revealed to him at this very moment. He was *feeling* the divine. The divine continued moving up his hands onto his arms. It slipped over his shirt sleeves, soaking through the fabric.

Rob wrinkled his nose. Gagged. The smell was too much to ignore now. The heavy scent of rotten eggs filled the cramped closet, assaulting his nose. He coughed and spluttered. Saliva dripped from his lips and fell into the fog.

RIP!

His button-up split down the middle, tearing off his body in the blink of an eye. The buttons popped off and clinked against the door in front of him. Fog swirled around his bare, hairy belly. He continued to retch, barely able to keep down the coffee and glazed donut he'd eaten that morning.

The wetness danced across his calves, snaking under his khakis. And then it tore his pants off, just like his shirt. The movement threw him off balance, sending him slamming into the closet door.

"Hey!"

The wetness continued up his legs. He cringed at the sensation and tried to shake it off. The wetness continued up to his tighty-whities, ripping the fabric easily, and sending his penis flopping limply into the cold foggy air. The wetness went upward, creeping up the backs of his hairy thighs and igniting goosebumps all over his body. Heat coasted over the back of his neck, burning his nose hairs with the horrible stench. It felt like an oversized dog was breathing on him.

Why, in God's name, was going to heaven so nightmarish? Was it the ultimate test of His follower's loyalty? Perhaps if they couldn't handle this last trial, they weren't worthy of seeing the kingdom of God?

He screamed as sharp pain erupted from his pointer finger. The wetness slipped under his fingernail, prying it up from the nail bed. He banged his hand against his thigh, desperately trying to throw the wetness off, but it had too firm of a grip. It continued, forcing his fingernail upward, bending it backward until it popped off. He screamed harder. More pain exploded at the end of his limbs as the wetness came for the rest of his fingernails and toenails.

He inhaled to scream again, but the wetness poured into his mouth, sucking out his breath and cutting off any sounds. It ripped out his right canine with a wet *pop*. He didn't even feel the pain before it yanked out the premolar beside it. Fiery pain exploded in his jaw. The wetness barreled on, separating his teeth from their rooted anchors with a surgical speed. Exposed nerves screamed in his mouth as the wetness mashed into them carelessly. It continued probing and pulling teeth. The grinding noise of snapping bone and tearing ligaments filled his ears, combining with the squelching of blood, saliva, and the cursed wetness. Blood choked his airway. He tried to breathe but only sucked down a molar fragment, slicing his esophagus open as his panicked lungs dragged it down his throat.

The wetness plunged into his asshole, tearing the skin. The wetness wasn't weak like a liquid; it was firm, plunging inside him with no forgiveness as it ripped its way up into his rectum. It thrusted in and out, moving faster and faster as blood and shit lubricated its path. The hot breath on the back of his neck doubled, coasting over him as the wetness destroyed his asshole.

His skull was on fire. His rectum felt as if it had turned into a gelatinous goo. And as the thing plunged deeper and deeper inside of him, fucking him well and good, he continued to wonder why getting to heaven took all of this pain and suffering? Perhaps it was to replicate Jesus's suffering on the cross.

Never once did the idea that he wasn't going to heaven cross his mind. Not even as he left the ground and his body rose into the air. His head slammed against the ceiling, and then he was out of the closet. Somewhere dark and cramped. And then the thing plunged further up his asshole, into his stomach, into his chest, and finally exploded out of his toothless mouth.

The world went black.

Mike kneeled on the ground, using a paper towel to sop up his spilled coffee. The congregation cheered and celebrated around him, panting and weary but all smiles. The lights had ceased flashing, and the fog had dissipated to a few thin wisps creeping around the baseboards.

Mike rubbed the sopping paper towel into the coffee-stained carpet with trembling hands. He shouldn't be surprised, but he always was. He never got used to the miracle Reverend Victor performed. He supposed it was his doubts that made him surprised when he saw it. But how could he doubt now? He had seen it happen right in front of him for the sixth time.

He looked up at the empty closet, desperately wishing to see Rob step out of it. The closet remained empty, the light bulb swinging. Mike almost looked away, but something caught his eye. Something underneath the bottom shelf rolled in dust and cobwebs. A brown blob.

He squinted. Reverend Victor, not noticing Mike's eyeline, absentmindedly shut the door. Just before the door clicked on its hinges, Mike was able to make out what it was. He dropped the sopping paper towel. His jaw went slack.

It was Rob's toupee.

Two

MIKE LAY AWAKE IN bed, staring at the ceiling. It was al-most midnight, but sleep hadn't yet come. Not even close. The images from today were burned into his mind. Sunday nights were always uncomfortable, but usually, eventually, he could push thoughts of Reverend Victor's closet out of his mind long enough to fall asleep. Sleep was one of the rare times he *didn't* have to think about Reverend Victor and his ... miracle.

But the image of Rob's toupee sitting in the closet kept chasing away the sandman. Had he seen right? Or was it something else? Perhaps a roll of old, brown paper towels. Or a wadded-up choir robe that had fallen out of place when Rob went up to heaven.

These rationalizations did nothing to make Mike sleepier. He knew damn well that it was Rob's toupee.

He rolled over and clamped his eyes shut, muttering a quick prayer, asking God to let sleep come and wash these thoughts away. The prayer seemed to do the opposite. His head flooded with questions.

Why was his toupee left behind? Why didn't it go to heaven?

Mike knew there ought to be a good, religious answer: we don't need our earthly possessions in heaven, simple as that. But if that was the case, why wasn't there a pile of clothes left in the closet every time Reverend Victor sent someone to heaven?

Why hadn't Rob's been left behind? What about anything he had in his pockets?

Every person who'd been taken before Rob had left no trace. Why had Rob? Did God simply forget it? Did he make a mistake and drop it as he was picking Rob up?

Mike's eyes snapped open. He sighed and sat up. No, that couldn't be it. God was utterly flawless.

And just like that, Mike was brought back to the question he'd been trying his damndest to avoid ever since Reverend Victor's first Sunday all those weeks ago:

What if those people aren't going to heaven?

Mike shuddered and slipped out of bed, grabbing his cigarettes from the nightstand before trotting down the stairs. He flicked on the kitchen light and lit up his cigarette, collecting a beer from the fridge as he took a long drag from the Pall Mall. He popped the tab on his beer and plopped into his cushy red recliner. The cold, malty liquid poured down his throat easily, kicking up his brain and getting him thinking.

Mike had always been the black sheep of the church world. Not only because of his inclination to Budweiser and swearing, but because he doubted. Deep down, he believed in God. He believed that Jesus Christ had died on the cross for the sins of the world, both past and future.

But whenever someone got into the nitty gritty specifics, there was always that little nagging in the back of his mind asking *how did that happen?* When Reverend Joe Mitchell, long before the molestation, had done a sermon series on Noah's Ark, Mike had struggled extra hard. He'd squirmed in the pew as Mitchell had droned on about how Noah loaded every single animal up on the boat in pairs.

Even flies? Mike thought. *There must be thousands of animals. How did they all get on that damn boat? How did none*

of them die? Why didn't the lion eat all the cows and knock the
zebras off the boat in the process? And say, why couldn't God
just give all those people, minus Noah and his family, a stroke?
Wouldn't that take care of the problem much faster?

Mike hated doubting God, but he had no control over the
thoughts. They sprouted in the back of his mind instantly,
nagging and tugging his shirt sleeve like a petulant child. He
realized that, at his core, he was just a suspicious type of
person. There was nothing he could do to stop it; he just had
to live with it.

He'd long dismissed the idea of leaving the faith completely. It had been his mother's staunch opinion that if your
ass wasn't planted firmly in a wooden pew come Sunday
morning; then you were no better than a communist. Mike's
mother, a 4'11 fireball of unbridled Appalachian energy, had
been lying six feet under at Oakwood Cemetery—God rest
her soul—for the past 7 years, but Mike didn't think he could
bring himself to soil her memory by leaving the church.

And even without his mother—he just *liked* the church.
The people there were nice, the songs were beautiful, and the
promise of an eternal reward grew more and more appealing
as Mike's hair continued to gray and his knees grew weaker.

And what would he have done after his surgery if Doris
and the Lady's Aid hadn't been at his door with a week's
worth of casseroles? How would he be spending his time
post-retirement without Bingo nights, Sunday service, and
breakfasts with Doug? Without a wife, children, siblings,
or any family minus his long-deceased mother, Oakwood
Baptist was the only family Mike had.

So, he had learned to live with his doubts. He allowed them
to sprout; there was no stopping that, but as soon as they reared
their ugly green heads, he took a mental weedeater to them.

He believed in God as a continued, deliberate choice, and his doubts hadn't been able to take that away from him.

But now, there was one doubt he couldn't chop down. One he had tried to shake but had clung firmly to the back of his skull, only growing louder and louder every passing Sunday until it was practically screaming at him.

THOSE PEOPLE AREN'T GOING TO HEAVEN! ROB'S TOUPEE IS EVIDENCE OF THAT!!! BRRRING! BRRRING! BRRRING!

The implications of this thought were catastrophic. He didn't even want to dare think of the ramifications were it true. Was Reverend Victor a misguided fool, unintentionally feeding people to an unfortunately placed sinkhole? Or was he sinister, perhaps a demon sent from hell to tempt people into following teachings not found in the Bible—and let that be clear, there were *no* teachings of supply closets that sent people to heaven in the Bible—and those who fell for the teachings got sucked straight to hell?

Mike found the idea that Reverend Victor was misguided the most believable, but they all sounded ludicrous. But so did the reverend's claim that those people were going to heaven …

He knocked back another swig of beer. Why did everyone believe the reverend so easily? Sure, they'd *seen* him send people away. But they didn't *know* that those people had been sent to heaven. They'd just vanished in a puff of fog. Mike had seen scantily clad women do the same thing on those magician specials on TV.

But, of course, the congregation believed Reverend Victor. They *loved* Reverend Victor. The fervent, blind adoration had been instant. Mike had never been a fan of the way the church worshiped the pastor, treating him as if he were the second coming of Jesus Christ. That made the doubts even more difficult to grapple with. Say he decided those people weren't going to heaven. There was no way anyone would believe him. Not without hard proof. And how on earth could he get hard proof in a scenario like this?

He finished his beer and crushed his cigarette. He'd brought himself to the same conclusion he'd reached every other time he pondered this topic. It was best to be ignored like all his other doubts. He climbed back up the stairs and lay back on his bed, hoping for the beer to lull him to sleep.

As soon as he closed his eyes, the image of Rob's toupee popped into his mind. He opened his eyes and sighed. He'd been able to shut down many doubts over the years.

But this one he had to get an answer to.

He slipped out of bed, taking off his pajamas and pulling on the pants he'd worn to church, hastily dressing before he could talk himself out of it. This was something he *had* to know.

He trotted downstairs and rummaged around in his junk drawer until he found a flickery old flashlight. He grabbed his keys and then stepped out onto the porch. Brisk, summer night air danced across his face. The urge to turn right around and climb back into his bed bubbled up in his stomach.

But he just wanted to see if it was Rob's toupee. After he confirmed it wasn't, he'd be done. He'd go back to ignoring his doubts and enjoying the spectacle every Sunday like the rest of the congregation.

He bustled down to his car and dropped himself into the driver's seat, cranking the key. The engine roared to life. Headlights blasted against his house. The gospel radio station he stayed tuned to began playing softly through his crackling speakers.

He rarely drove through Oakwood at night. It felt strange. The gas stations he usually passed in the morning sun were glowing with neon lights. Restaurants he normally saw populated by people his age overflowed with teenagers and young adults.

He rolled down Walsh Street, passing Tim's house. A for-sale sign was stuck in the grass. Of course, it wasn't Tim's house anymore. Tim had gone to heaven at the beginning of Reverend Victor's tenure. And boy, did Mike miss the guy. They'd been friends for decades, even gone to school with each other when they were boys.

Then Tim got prostate cancer. The poor fella had been in a bit of pain from the treatments, so when the reverend who claimed the ability to send people to heaven painlessly showed up ...

There had been no funeral, no mourning, and no conversations about how much the church missed him. Tim was just gone.

See, that's another thing, Mike thought. *Reverend Victor said that the purpose of the closet was to send the terminally ill, elderly beyond hope, and those without a quality of life to heaven with dignity.*

But that hadn't lasted. He'd worked through those with illnesses within the first couple weeks, leaving only *extremely* old, but generally healthy people to pick from. And then people like Rob had been sent to heaven. Rob whose only health issue was his male-pattern-baldness.

Trees replaced houses and stores as Mike got closer to the church. His palms coated the steering wheel with a glossy sheen of sweat. His stomach twisted itself into knots.

The way he saw it, there were two outcomes of this brief trip to the church. One, he'd go downstairs, find no trace of Rob's toupee, feel like an idiot, and head home with his tail tucked between his legs. This would be the best outcome, even if it wouldn't *fully* get rid of his doubts. Nothing could do that, but it'd ease them enough for him to fall asleep.

But if he found the toupee ... well, that would change some things.

The church came into view, nestled in the trees, the parsonage a few hundred feet beside it. Mike rolled into the parking lot, pulling into the spot closest to the oak double doors. He leaned forward, staring out the window at the building. It looked even worse at night. The shadows from the many chips and dings in the wood were much sharper; the paint looked even more peeling and old.

Mike took a deep breath and stepped out. The stench was present as ever, souring in his lungs. He ignored his itch for a cigarette and began shuffling up to the porch steps. His hands trembled as he stepped onto the rickety porch, provoking a long *creeeaaak.* He reached forward and grabbed the cold steel door handle, twisting it and pulling. The door hinges whined as it came open. Hot, stinky air poured forward, rushing over his face and making him cringe.

"Motherfucker," Mike muttered. He had been uneasy the whole drive, but was surprised to find just how scared he was. His heart hammered in his chest, and his stomach was twisting itself into knots. He hadn't been scared like this since he was a boy crippled with stage fright about to sing in the school play.

And just like when he was a boy, the only way to get over fear was to do what was making you scared. He stepped a foot into the church, gingerly setting it on the cushy carpet. Chills raced up his arms. He followed with the other foot and allowed the door to click behind him, wrapping darkness around him. He itched to reach out to his right and flick on the overhead lights, but he worried that the light would reach the parsonage and wake Reverend Victor.

He mashed the switch on his flashlight. The dim line of light hardly chased away the thick, creeping dark surrounding him, only cutting through the middle, but it would have to do. Mike started forward, creeping along the creaky floors. Goddamn, churches were creepy at night. The pews and pulpit cast menacing shadows across the wood walls. Without the chatter of the congregation, he could hear every time the building settled; every individual click of the clocks.

He pulled open the door to the basement, the stench renewing and burning his nose hairs. He wrinkled his nose and pointed his flashlight down the narrow, carpeted steps. Everything inside of him begged him to turn back, to run to the car and speed home. Crawl in bed and forget about this whole thing.

You know damn well forgetting about this whole thing would be impossible.

He steeled himself and took a step down, doing it like he'd done at that school recital, only focusing on the very next step. One foot in front of the other.

The minuscule comfort of the moonlight seeping in through the stained-glass windows abandoned him as he descended deeper into the darkness. After what felt like forever, he reached the bottom and shined his flashlight on the basement.

Wood-paneled walls, gray carpet, white folding tables and chairs. Mike was grateful to reach over and turn on the overhead lights down here. No windows meant no chance of Reverend Victor seeing him.

Why are you so scared of him seeing you?

Mike ignored this thought and walked over to the small, dingy closet sitting on the other side of the basement. He approached it cautiously, as if any second it'd swing open and suck him up to heaven, hell, or some weird place in between. It did no such things, even as he got close enough to run his fingers over the course, hollow, plywood door.

Could this little closet be a gateway to the divine? Mike knew he'd all but seen it—but damn it, he still couldn't bring himself to fully believe it. He twisted the knob with a clammy hand, pulling the door open. For the third time, the stench increased. This time, enough to make him cough. He reached up and tugged on the chain, turning on the bulb and sending it swinging. Orange light glowed over the shelves. Mike crouched and looked under the bottom shelf. His heart flipped in his chest, even though he'd seen it this morning.

He reached under and pulled out Rob's toupee, shaking off the dust.

God in heaven, where are you, Rob?

Fear spread through Mike's veins like poison, and he wanted to drop the toupee and sprint back the way he'd come. But he also wanted answers. He wanted to know why Rob's toupee was here. Mike stood, examining every inch of the closet, still clutching the hairpiece. His eyes raked over spider webs, broken Christmas lights, dusty bottles of pine-sol, moth-eaten choir robes, and old moldy pew cushions. There was nothing that would indicate a portal to heaven.

Mike continued to look, rummaging through the boxes and scouring the shelves. He didn't know what he was looking for, and whatever it was, he didn't find it. He stepped back from the closet after 20 minutes of searching, sweaty, frustrated, and still clutching the hairpiece.

He kicked the door shut in frustration. The loud bang made him cringe, but it also made him think back to this morning when Reverend Victor had slammed his hands against the door. Just like he always did ... Mike paused. Maybe ...

He lifted his hands—flashlight in one, Rob's toupee in the
other—and smacked them against the door. Once, twice, thrice,
four times. The door rattled in its hinges with each impact.
Mike hesitated before the fifth impact. The church had fallen
unnaturally silent. His mouth had gone dry. His curiosity won
out, and he slammed his hands into the door for one final, fifth
time.

He ripped the door open, taking a step back and watching
with wide eyes.

Nothing happened.

He inched forward, peering inside. It was the same closet as
before. He didn't know what he expected to see. God's hand
reaching from the ceiling and groping around for some random
congregation member?

HISSS!

"Holy hell!" Mike roared, throwing himself backward and
landing flat on his ass. Fog shot from the cracks in the closet
ceiling, cresting down like a slow-motion waterfall. The lights
flickered on and off above him.

The stench came on stronger than he'd ever smelled it. It
smelled like garbage. Sulfur. *Rot.* His eyes watered. It ripped a
gag from his throat. His stomach clenched painfully, threaten-
ing to eject the beer he'd drunk before coming over.

"By God," Mike groaned.

He forced his tear-filled eyes open and watched through his
retching as the closet filled with smoke.

Shuffleshuffleshuffle.

The noise of movement came from the closet. Mike whimpered and began scooting backward in a hasty crab walk. The
fog loomed out after him, beginning to coast across the floor.
He scrambled to his feet, dropping the flashlight, dropping the
toupee.

Something flew from the closet, arcing out of the fog and landing at Mike's feet with a thick *splat*. Mike looked down to see a mangled, degloved penis and testicles. Without the skin, the wet, pale organ looked like something you'd buy at a butcher's shop. One testicle was smashed as flat as a pancake, oozing blood.

"Christ!"

He knew it was Rob's penis. He knew it like he knew the sky was blue.

That's Rob's dick. That's his fucking chopped-off dick lying on the carpet in front of me. He's dead, and somebody done went and chopped off his cock! And they threw it right at me!

The stench and sight of the mangled genitals were too much. Mike clutched his stomach and vomited, spraying his dinner and beer across the carpet. Even while he was puking his guts out, a very distinct and clear thought came to the front of his mind.

I need to get out of here.

He spun around, his brown dress shoes squelching in the vomit. He sprinted toward the stairs, kicking up the fog. Even though he was getting farther from the closet, the stench was only growing—attacking his nose and throat, making him gag and splutter. He threw himself up the stairs, his shoes leaving slick trails of his vomit on the steps. He stumbled halfway up, bashing his knees into the stairs, but wasted no time, immediately throwing himself back to his feet and scrambling the rest of the way.

He burst into the sanctuary, sprinting down the dark room and—*"COCKSUCKER, FUCK!"*

—bashing his leg into the pew. His shin collided with the wood, sending sharp, jolting pain rocketing up his shin. He slammed into the carpet, clutching his leg and groaning.

No time, no time, no time.

He ignored the throbbing pain. He ignored the painful pulse of his heart in his throat. He ignored the acrid taste of vomit on his tongue. He ignored the damn rotten stench in his nose. He hoisted himself to his feet, wincing at the stabbing pain from putting weight on his leg. He returned to a sprint, running blindly until he burst through the double doors.

The fresh summer air—now seeming only mildly tainted by the stench after what he'd smelled in the basement—poured into his sinuses. He didn't stop running. He streaked down the steps and hooked a hard right, gunning straight for the parsonage. If he'd been thinking straight, he might have re-considered going straight to Reverend Victor, but the stench and the sight of the mangled penis addled his mind. Reverend Victor's house represented another person. And damn it, Mike needed another person.

He sprinted through the slick grass, leaping up on the porch of the small, one-story house. He hammered his fist into the door and jammed his finger on the doorbell.

"Reverend! Reverend Victor!" Mike yelled. He continued hammering away on the door and mashing the doorbell but got no answer. His heart hammered in his chest. His head felt light and fuzzy. Was the reverend out? God, he hoped not.

He whipped his head over to the driveway. The reverend's souped-up 1982 Cadillac Fleetwood Brougham—a car that had to cost at least $20,000—was still in the driveway. Mike whimpered and began pounding his fist on the door again.

"Reverend, *please, please, please!*" He shouted.

The porch light turned on. Relief crashed through Mike. A second later, the door creaked open, revealing Reverend Victor wearing only striped pajama pants, his bare chest gleaming with sweat. The reverend frowned, harsh shadow lines cast on his face from the porch light.

"What the hell is going on?" he said.

Mike shoved past the reverend, pushing inside, tripping on the lip of the doorway and landing flat on his stomach inside the foyer.

"Mike! What are ya doin'?" The reverend said.

Mike leaped back up to his feet; his vision went blurry, and his head filled with fuzz as he stood up. "Help. I need ... I need cops ... ambulance—*something*."

"Ambulance? Cops? Mike, what the hell are you talking about?!"

Mike opened his mouth to speak, but the fuzz in his head was only growing. Reverend Victor became a blurry blob, and then darkness crept around the corner of his vision. Mike slumped to the ground and passed out.

THREE

CONSCIOUSNESS CREPT BACK TO Mike. The cold tile of Reverend Victor's floor pressed against his head. His right shin sent sharp stabs of pain pulsing through his leg. The pain grew as he became more alert. And he began hearing voices, murky and dull at first but growing sharper and sharper.

"... you sure you don't want me to call the police?" a female voice said. Mike felt confused why he was hearing a woman's voice.

"Naw, I'll take care of it. You go on," Reverend Victor said.

The sound of Reverend Victor's voice brought back the memories of what had just happened in full force, pushing away any of Mike's curiosity about who the woman was. Mike peeled his eyes open and shoved himself into a seated position as her footsteps battered back down the hallway.

"Reverend, we—"

Reverend Victor held up a hand. "Mike, calm down. Speak with *words*."

Mike took a deep breath. Swallowed. The taste of vomit was thick on his tongue. "I went over to the church. Into the basement. And I saw... something horrible."

What had he seen? How could he describe it to Reverend Victor? A dismembered penis with no skin falling from the roof in the closet where people were allegedly sent to heaven?

Reverend Victor's eyebrows furrowed. "What kind of something horrible?"

"Somebody's ... *penis.*" Mike didn't tell him he thought—no, *knew*—it was Rob's. If Mike's theory that the reverend was not aware of the ramifications of his actions was true, he would need to be eased into this. "It was chopped off. Laying in the closet."

Reverend Victor's face hardened. "Did you hit your head, Mike?"

"What? No."

"You're not making sense."

"No. *No.* I saw it. I swear to God," Mike said. He struggled up and slumped into a kitchen chair. His whole body felt incredibly sweaty. Reverend Victor studied him, his facial expression unreadable.

"Mike, you're talking crazy," Reverend Victor said.

Mike sucked in more air. God*damn,* he wanted a cigarette. "Before my God, I promise you I saw it."

Reverend Victor rubbed a hand over his tan face. It was almost strange to see the Reverend without an abundance of jewelry. "Show me then."

Mike's stomach dropped. He had been expecting they would hunker down behind locked doors and call the police. "You want to go back there?"

Reverend Victor placed a hand on his shoulder. "Well, if what you're saying is true, we can't just leave a mangled cock on the floor, now can we? Do you think old Henrietta wants to see that this Sunday? Come on, Mike, show me where ya found it."

Reverend Victor didn't pull on a shirt or grab a pair of shoes, he just pushed open the screen door and struck off into the summer night.

"Shitfire," Mike muttered, hoisting himself to his feet and following his pastor. The thick, silent air outside raised goosebumps on Mike's skin. Reverend Victor marched across the grass with his chest puffed out. Mike had to speed-walk to keep up with the Reverend's long strides. A thick ball of dread built up in his stomach, growing more and more the closer they got to the church. The idea of again stepping foot in the building made him want to throw up. And he *would* throw up if that stench got as strong as it had in the basement.

Reverend Victor walked up the porch steps, his bare feet slapping on the wood. He pushed open the doors to the church. Mike's stomach lurched at the increasing stench. He pulled himself up the steps, cringing at the aches and pains all over his body. The pulsing pain from his shin told him he'd have a nasty bruise to look at.

Reverend Victor turned the overhead lights on, making it a tad easier for Mike to step foot inside. Still, he felt about as comfortable as he would sticking his hand down the garbage disposal. Reverend Victor paid no mind to Mike's trepidation, charging for the gaping basement door.

"Reverend, what if someone's down there?" Mike said, his voice high.

"Well, we can't let 'em spend the night," Reverend Victor said, descending the stairs.

Mike wanted to say more. Somehow, convince the reverend that they should not take this so lightly. But words failed, and the back of Reverend Victor's head disappeared down the stairs. Mike didn't want to go into the basement, but he damn well didn't want to be alone in the church either, so he hurried after the pastor, forcing himself down the stairs the same way he'd done it not even an hour ago: one step at a time.

The lights hummed as they reached the basement. The stench was still rancid and heavy in the air, but it was no longer so over-powering that Mike felt he would vomit. The fog had dissipated. He raked his eyes over the walls, the floor, and especially the closet, ready to sprint back up the stairs at the first sign of danger. His face flushed as he and Reverend Victor both caught sight of his pile of vomit.

"Where's the pecker?" Reverend Victor grunted.

Mike pointed toward the closet. The door was still ajar, and the light bulb still glowed. His finger faltered in the air. The penis was gone. Not even a bloodstain remained on the carpet where it had plopped.

"Right ... right there," Mike said.

Reverend Victor turned to him, a suave, comforting facial expression pulled across his features. "Churches can be scary at night, can't they? You probably got real spooked and imagined it."

"No! No, I saw it—I know I did," Mike said.

"There ain't no shame in gettin' scared, Mike. It happens to all of us. It was probably a trick of the light," Reverend Victor said.

Mike clenched his fists, feeling like a stupid little kid dismissed by his parents. He knew damn well that he hadn't imagined it, but stammering and pleading with the reverend wouldn't do him any good. He looked over at the closet again.

"Was *this* a trick of the light?" Mike said, darting to the closet and picking up the brown blob that was Rob's toupee.

Mike saw the charming preacher's facade slip. Reverend Victor's face paled. He stomped over to Mike and snatched the wig from him. "Where'd you get this?"

"It was in the closet this morning after Rob went to heaven. It's his hairpiece."

"I know what it is," Reverend Victor snapped. He examined the hairpiece in his hands like it was some sort of alien device. Mike saw the angry confusion on Reverend Victor's face fade and give way to the same sanitized, cheerful, and endearing face that Reverend Victor wore constantly.

"Yes, it looks like Rob's. One of his earthly possessions left behind." Reverend Victor turned to Mike, smiling a politician grin. "Suppose we don't need things like this up there, do we?"

Mike felt frustration building inside of him. "I think it was Rob's... member, I saw."

Reverend Victor scoffed, but Mike had to get this out. He *had* to tell someone else. This wasn't a weed of doubt he could just snip off.

"His hairpiece was left behind, and then I swear on my mother that I saw a di—piece of genitalia in the closet and..." Mike suddenly had such a powerful surge of emotions he felt like crying. He forced back tears and plowed on. "Reverend, I *worry* sometimes. It's not that I doubt you or the Lord, but... but... damn it, sometimes I wonder what if the people aren't going to heaven—"

Reverend Victor's fist collided with Mike's jaw. Stars exploded in his head. He slammed into the wall beside the closet, slumping down to the carpet, pain blossoming in the side of his face. He looked up with damp eyes. Reverend Victor glared down at him. The saccharine smile was gone. His face was completely neutral. His eyes conveyed no emotion.

"Never say some stupid shit like that again, you hear me?"

His voice sounded more plain, too. His southern twang, while still present, didn't punctuate his words like it usually did.

Mike croaked.

"Promise me you won't say any more of that bullshit," Reverend Victor said.

"I ..."

Reverend Victor struck Mike—hard. The slap of his palm against Mike's cheek boomed around the basement. Mike clutched his face. It felt like a thousand bees were stinging him.

"Say you *won't*," Reverend Victor spat, leaning over Mike until their noses were a hair away from touching.

Mike had never been one to succumb to bullies. Lance Walden had tried to take his lunch money back in grade school, and even though Mike was a scrawny little twerp, he had taken on Lance Morgan right in the recess yard. He even got in a punch right to Lance's gut. Of course, Mike had received two black eyes, a busted nose, and bruises all up and down his body. But Lance had never tried for his money again. Even as a kid, Mike knew instinctively that it was *always* the better option to stand up to a bully. It was a good philosophy and one he'd always abided by at many points in his life.

But something about Reverend Victor broke that part of Mike. He cowered under the man's shadow, scrunching himself as tight as he could get against the wall.

"I won't," he said.

Reverend Victor ground his teeth, exhaling in slow, calculated breaths, beaming the scent of spearmint tic-tacs into Mike's nose. Sweat dripped from his brow. He stared at Mike a little longer, his eyes empty, before stepping back. He flipped over the toupee in his hands, examining it again.

"No ... this isn't Rob's ... you were mistaken," he said.

"You said it was," Mike said before he could stop himself.

Reverend Victor's face lit with emotion—pure, uncontrolled rage. His eyes popped. Veins bulged on his neck. His eyebrows shot up into his hairline.

"No, I did not—and don't you *ever say I did!*" he spat, waving a finger in Mike's face.

Mike shrunk even further under this sudden outburst of rage. His lips welded themselves shut. His hands trembled in fear, not of what was in the closet but of the man towering over him.

Reverend Victor took a step back, clutching the wig in his fist. He glanced over at the pile of Mike's vomit. "Go get some paper towels. Clean that shit up. I don't want anyone to know anything about tonight. You understand me?"

Mike nodded, his teeth chattering together. He stood, ignoring the throb in his jaw and the pain in his leg. He slunk past Reverend Victor like a kicked dog and collected a roll of paper towels from the basement bathroom. The reverend stood over him as he scraped his already-drying puke up off the carpet, gathering big gobs of it in the paper towels. He trembled as he worked.

The trip had been a nightmare, but it hadn't been a failure. There were two facts he knew for certain now.

One, those people were not going to heaven. *Had* not gone to heaven. Wherever Rob had disappeared to this morning in a gust of fog had not been to the pearly gates. He had no clue where they were going—or what nightmarish secrets that closet might hold—but he knew it was not heaven.

And two, Reverend Victor knew he wasn't sending them to heaven.

And he didn't want anyone else to know.

Vanessa lay sprawled in Reverend Victor's bed—the pastor's cum drying on her stomach—waiting for him to return. God, what a lovely time they'd been having. She hadn't had so much fun fucking since she and Rob were in college. She was just about to have her first orgasm of the night when Mike came bursting in, talking a bunch of gibberish. Rob had always liked Mike, but Vanessa had found the scrawny, gray-haired fella to be annoying.

His crying to her fuckbuddy like a kid wanting his daddy to check for monsters under the bed worsened this impression.

Vanessa hoped the reverend would return soon. She no longer had the stamina she'd possessed in her sorority days but would like to get one off before she fell asleep.

She scanned the room to keep her eyes from fluttering closed. Hoping to find some cute pictures of the reverend in his younger days, she only found empty walls and stacks of packages. God, lots of packages. The reverend got so much damn mail, but he didn't even open most of it. Her eyes wandered to the nightstand. A pack of condoms, a pile of receipts, dozens of thick gold rings, gold chains, gold watches, and a squat brown lamp that bathed the room in moody orange light.

Although cluttered, the room still felt barren. Impermanent. Reverend Victor had been the pastor for, what was it, 3 months now? Surely, he'd had plenty of time to move in. He'd certainly had time to move into her pants.

She laid contentedly back, her long blonde hair splayed on the pillow. She brought the pastor's blankets up, covering her breasts. Of course, she wasn't the only one he saw. *Many* of the women at Oakwood Baptist had... fantasies about Reverend Victor. And as long as you were pretty enough, you could count on making those fantasies a reality. She often wondered how many of their husbands knew about their pastor's inclination toward their wives.

Rob had been aware. They'd never openly talked about it, but all the same, they'd both known and they'd both known the *other* knew. It just had changed nothing. Sure, if it had been any other man, Rob would've been irate. Probably would've beaten her.

But it wasn't just any other man... it was *Reverend Victor*.

There was something special about that man. He wasn't some weak, namby-pamby pastor who blabbered about God's love on Sunday and then sat with his thumb up his ass the rest of the week. No, he *did* what all pastors said they were gonna do. He made sure his congregation went to heaven. But not just by leading them to live pious lives. No, he had a rapport with God. Could send people straight up to heaven.

One of the main reasons that Vanessa had finally given in to the affair was her not having to worry about going to hell for her infidelity. She could choke on the reverend's dick all she wanted, and when her time came, he could just load her up in the closet and beam her up.

The bedroom door clicked open. She sat up, letting the blanket fall and pushing her breasts out.

"Welcome back."

Reverend Victor grunted, shuffling to the closet. He pulled it open, shuffling around with some more cardboard boxes.

"I need to get you a dresser," Vanessa teased.

Reverend Victor chuckled, emerging from the closet. "Don't need one."

Vanessa's eyes darted down to the leather straps he was now holding. "What have we here?"

Reverend Victor grinned. "Let's have a little fun, huh, pretty thing?"

Vanessa squealed with glee, eagerly allowing her pastor to wrap the leather restraints around her ankles and then her wrists.

"Who knew a pastor could be so *bad?*" she teased.

Reverend Victor smiled at her. "One more thing."

He produced a black blindfold. She shuddered with antici-pation as he delicately wrapped it around her head. She lay back on the bed, desperate for his touch.

"What are you going to do to me?" she whispered. She craved his hands over her—*inside* of her. He wasn't that sexually skilled, nor was he well endowed, but there was something *about* him. Maybe it was his power. Maybe it was the fact that other women desired him. She didn't know, nor did she care.

She felt his penis stab at her lips. Obediently, she opened her mouth, accepting it in, moaning around it. He thrust into her mouth, grunting and panting, until he burst a feeble old man's load onto her tongue. She swallowed it gratefully.

"Give me more," she whispered. She waited with bated breath, eager for whatever sexual contact Reverend Victor would bless her with next.

A sour, chemical smell filled her nose. Stickiness covered her lips. She hummed against the duct tape now on her mouth. Horniness flushed through her. What sort of carnal things would the reverend do to her with the tape over her mouth?

The hammer smashed into her ankle, shattering bone and sending her foot into an unnatural angle. Pain exploded in her leg and ripped up her body, pulling a raw scream from her throat. She bellowed against the tape, her cry of agony muffled.

"Sorry, honey. I can't have you trying to run," Reverend Vic-tor cooed, using the same tone of voice he used when he talked dirty to her.

Tears streamed down Vanessa's face. She thrashed on the bed. She tried to lift herself, but the restraints on her legs and wrists held her firm. The hammer hit her other ankle, mirroring the excruciating pain. She wailed again, pulling her wrists at the restraints desperately. It served only to cut the leather deep into her skin.

And then Reverend Victor was picking her up. He threw her over his shoulders like she was a sack of potatoes. She shook her head, trying to get the blindfold off, but it was tied too tight. She tried to ask him where he was taking her, but between her sobbing and the tape, it came out as a disconnected jumble.

He seemed to get the idea, though.

"I'm sorry to do this so soon. I meant to keep you around a little longer, but Mike got it all riled up," Reverend Victor drawled.

Vanessa had no clue what Mike had to do with this, but she realized that this wasn't just some elaborate kink the reverend had. She was in mortal danger.

She thrashed and kicked on his shoulder, screaming against the tape as best she could. She kept writhing even as he took her outside. The jostling of movement and late-night, summer wind seemed to aggravate her painful, broken ankles. They felt utterly demolished. She shuddered to think what they would look like.

By the warm rush of air and the scent of old wood, Vanessa could tell they were inside the church now.

What in God's name are we doing here?!

She heard a door swing open. Then she felt the Reverend and her descend.

The basement? What are we ... he's not going to ... he isn't gonna send me to heaven, is he?

Vanessa slackened a little. Her panic subsided a bit. Things could be *worse*. She had expected Reverend Victor to rape and kill her—but if he was just sending her to heaven, well, that wouldn't be so bad, would it? No, of course not! It was heaven!

Vanessa had no issue leaving her life here on earth, even though she enjoyed it very much. But why would she care about this life when a flawless one in heaven awaited her? If anything—she wondered why she hadn't *asked* Reverend Victor to go to heaven sooner.

She heard the closet door open. Reverend Victor dumped her inside. She landed hard—her bare ass hitting the carpet with a thud and her mangled ankles knocking painfully into the doorway. She let out a choked sob.

"Enjoy heaven, Vanessa. Say hi to Rob for me," Reverend Victor said.

The door slammed. Then she heard five slams against the door. And then—footsteps. Retreating. Reverend Victor leaving.

In all the times Vanessa had imagined being sent to heaven, the church had always been present. It felt strange to have the fantasy realized, but without her church family here to witness it.

And how was she to go to heaven in this state? Naked, covered in cum. She swallowed, growing nervous again. What if God saw the state she was in and declined her entry, tossing her back to earth? What if she sat in this closet until next Sunday?

HISS!

Her panic subsided as the familiar fog filled in around her. She lay her head back against the wall, waiting for the divine to sweep her away. Of course, she should've known better than to even think about doubting Reverend Victor, even if he had broken her ankles.

The stench she had dutifully ignored for 3 months became too much to bear. She puked immediately, her mouth filling with vomit as she desperately fumbled her hands up to her mouth and ripped off the tape. Then the wetness came. She screamed as each finger and toenail was plucked from her appendages; she howled as her teeth were ripped from her mouth.

But she made no noises as she was sucked into the air.

Four

Mike strolled into Clive's, forcing a smile. Clive's was the designated pre-church breakfast spot of Oakwood Baptist. Every Sunday, more than half of the congregation shuffled in and parked their butts in red vinyl booths to enjoy toasted waffles, fluffy pancakes, and bacon dripping with grease.

This Sunday was no different. Just before 9:00 in the morning, the congregation had their arms resting on sticky tables as they ate and chatted about the upcoming church service. The thick scent of coffee and maple syrup filled the air, but Mike's stomach had been tied in a knot since last week, and he didn't feel like eating. He managed to smile and nod to his church family as he walked to the table in the back.

It had been one week since his encounter in the basement and the subsequent encounter with Reverend Victor and all the knowledge he'd gained from it. And it had been a miserable week, filled with tension and sleepless nights, clutching his blankets and staring at the ceiling with wide eyes as his mind forced him to wonder what on God's beautiful green earth was in that closet.

His mind always came up blank. It could conjure up some horrible images—demons waiting in the floorboards, ax murderers in the walls, the devil himself opening his gaping mouth to swallow up the foolish congregation—but he could never picture something that made sense. He had no clue what was in that closet, if it was sentient or not, if it was sending those people somewhere or just killing them.

And that was even scarier than if he'd just seen a monster.

When he wasn't trying to put that puzzle together, he was racking his brain for a solution. *Something* would need to be done, even if he didn't know the details of the closet yet. His first idea, and it had seemed a pretty damn good one, was to flee. Make out like a bat outta hell and leave Oakwood, the church, and that closet with its tendency to chuck flayed cocks on the floor, all in the dust. He'd gotten so far as to pack a suitcase and drive over to Smokin' Steven's and fill up his car with gas. But after driving past the entrance ramp to the highway three times, he'd driven back home.

The only thing stopping him from burning rubber and tearing down the road with a parting middle finger toward Reverend Victor was his total lack of a destination. Where was he to go? He had no living family to flock to. He had no friends out of state he could couch surf with. Not even a wife and kids to take with him for company. What good would it do to run out his retirement savings in a motel two states over?

This confirmed his worry that Oakwood Baptist was all he had. The congregation was the closest thing resembling a family to him. And that brought with it another point—if these people were his family, how could he abandon them to whatever horrible fate Reverend Victor had for them in that closet? Guilt stabbed at him for how easily he would've left them all behind if he'd only had somewhere to go.

He couldn't leave. Neither practically nor morally. And goddamn did that make him feel trapped.

The second option was to tell someone. Mike found that to be the most logical of the two. Sitting on the knowledge would make him an accomplice to murder—

Is it murder? Are they dying? Where are they going? You don't lose your cock without dying, right?

—and no better than just abandoning the church. But who could he tell?

He let his eyes roll over the members of Oakwood Baptist as he walked over the checkered floors. You could immediately tell an Oakwood Baptist member from another patron. Their eyes were hazy, seeming to be focused on everything in the room and nothing at all. They chomped on their food with open mouths, spraying mushy bits of biscuits onto the arms of their breakfast partners, who didn't seem to notice. And their conversations—the snippets Mike overheard as he passed—were fixed on one topic: Reverend Victor.

"... so much better now, thanks to him ..."

"...—inally cleaning up that mess Joe Mitchell left him ..."

"... I haven't connected with a pastor like this before. I feel for him. I do ..."

The thought of levying an accusation with the weight of the one Mike had loaded on his tongue was daunting. It made his pits sweat to imagine what would happen if he stood up one Sunday and loudly proclaimed to the whole church that Reverend Victor was a heretic.

No one would believe him. They cared too much for the reverend. They'd whip themselves up into a frenzy and throw Mike out of the church.

He'd have to target people individually. Still, that wouldn't be much easier. He'd never heard a negative word against Reverend Victor from any single member of the congregation.

Mike spotted Doug at their usual booth in the back corner. The two men waved, and Mike strolled over, plopping himself across from his buddy. Doug was as big of a Reverend Victor fan as anybody in the church, but he was also Mike's friend.

Had been for years. When Doug's wife had endured a brutal, months-long battle with breast cancer that had ultimately taken her life, Mike had been there for Doug more than anyone. That had to count for something, didn't it?

"Morning," Doug said, flapping his menu like a newspaper.

Mike nodded. "Morning."

Doug was a squat man in overalls with a pair of Coke-bottle glasses balancing on his nose. Even through the glasses, Mike could tell his eyes weren't as focused as they'd once been. Even though he'd been sporting a thick wooden cane for years, Doug had always been sharp as a tack. Until recently. Until Reverend Victor came to town.

Doug had been Mike's closest friend in the church ever since Tim had gone to heaven. If there was anyone who would hear him out, it would be Doug.

They fell into their usual small talk, discussing the weather and sports with all the enthusiasm of two men out fishing. The waitress came and took their order, and within ten minutes, they had their breakfasts in front of them. Mike sipped his coffee while Doug sliced into his pancakes. Mike knew he needed to tell Doug what he'd seen, but he had no idea how to even begin that conversation.

"Wonder what the sermon will be about today," he said.

Doug shrugged, forking half an egg into his mouth. "Dunno. It'll be great, though."

Mike nodded, even though he had found none of Reverend Victor's sermons great.

"I just hope he picks me to go to heaven soon. My knees have been killing me," Doug said.

Mike forced himself to keep a straight face. It had been 3 months of insane statements like this, but Mike had yet to grow used to them. How had they so quickly reached the point where

Doug was now welcoming what was effectively euthanasia because his knee was acting up?

"You don't want to have breakfast with me a few more times before you head up?" Mike said, trying to sound casual.

Doug looked at him blankly. "It's heaven. Don't you wanna go?"

Mike bit his lip. He needed to choose his answers carefully because hell NO, he did not want to step foot in that closet. But Doug couldn't know that.

"When the good Lord calls me," he said.

"Reverend Victor only sends people when God calls them," Doug said.

"I wonder why the Lord doesn't just ... take us in our sleep like he used to do," Mike said, trying to strike a tone of curiosity rather than accusatory. He sliced a bit of pancake and popped it into his mouth, trying to appear casual.

Doug looked up, frowning. "Reverend Victor explained this a while back. Our church did things real good—just how God likes 'em—for so long that the Lord blessed us with Reverend Victor. And he can send people to heaven so they don't have to go through a suffering death."

Mike thought it sounded even stupider coming from Doug. Reverend Victor was charismatic enough to couch the idea in enough suave rhetoric so that you almost forgot what you were hearing. But the concept so plainly explained by Doug's ineloquent tongue sounded like complete gibberish.

"Mmm," Mike said.

"What? You'd rather have a heart attack on the commode?" Doug chuckled.

Mike smiled. "No, of course not, I'm very grateful for this blessing from the Lord it's just ..." He better rip the bandaid off. "I worry about some of the other people in our church."

Doug stopped cutting a sausage link. "Oh?"

Mike nodded. "I heard some people chatting the other day. They were wondering if ... if maybe Reverend Victor was misguided and *wasn't* sending people to heaven." He vomited the sentence out quickly.

Doug's pudgy fist clenched around his fork. Veins bulged on his neck. His face flushed as red as the booth they were sitting in, and his eyes, normally glazed over like the rest of the church, burst alight with rage.

"Who said *that?*" he spat.

"I can't remember," Mike said quickly, trying as hard as he could to run to his point. "They were talking about Rob going to heaven. Turns out some people saw his toupee in the closet after he'd gone to heaven."

Doug wasn't registering the words. He steamed like a kettle. "Who said this shit, Mike?"

"I told you I don't know. But what do you think about Rob's toupee being left behind?" Mike said, desperately trying to prod Doug into looking past the critique of Reverend Victor and answering the question at hand.

Ragged, angry gasps were shooting out of Doug's flared nostrils. "If I get my hands on them."

"What about Rob's toupee?" Mike pressed.

"It's a goddamn lie, I'll tell you that! Something a twisted brain cooked up to turn us against God!" Doug roared, smashing his fists on the table and jostling their plates. Spit flew from his mouth, landing on Mike's pancakes.

Doug's behavior disturbed Mike. He'd only seen the congregation's adoration for Reverend Victor manifest in positive ways so far, and it filled his stomach with dread to know that the inverse was true. Mike had only insinuated there were rumors that perhaps Reverend Victor had been mistaken, and it had sent Doug into a fury.

They'd all act like this, Mike thought hopelessly.

"Doug, come to think of it, I think *I* might've seen the toupee, too," Mike said, pulling out all the stops.

"You were mistaken. You fell for the rumors. The *lies* on Reverend Victor's good name, damn it," Doug said.

Mike could tell that there was a wall in Doug's mind that could not be crossed. The conversation was pointless. Dead before it even started. Doug had no intention of hearing anything that contradicted a single word from Reverend Victor's mouth, and Mike knew Doug represented the opinions of everyone else in the church.

Mike needed proof. Without proof, it was his word against the reverend's. And they'd pick the reverend every time. Mike deflated as he realized that he'd *had* proof in the form of Rob's toupee but had let Reverend Victor carry it off last week. It was no doubt hidden or destroyed.

The topic of conversation shifted, turning to politics and television, though Doug kept interjecting comments about how great Reverend Victor was. Mike tuned out, letting Doug's words fade into an unintelligible *buzz.*

I'll find more proof, he thought. *I'll go back to that damn church tonight if I have to. Hell, I'll drag Doug out of bed and bring him to the basement. Let him smell the stench, see the dick, and tell me it's a portal to heaven.*

With most everyone's food done, tables mingled. Mike and Doug had several visitors wobble over to them on canes and walkers, old men and women all eager to talk about how great Reverend Victor's sermon would be.

Kirsty Johnson and her husband, Ted, came over. Ted was tall and bald, but had a face shaped like Kirsty's. They were one of those couples who looked more like siblings than spouses. Even if Ted wouldn't go to church with Kirsty, he often frequented Clive's before dropping his wife and son off.

Ted—eyes sharp as ever, not infected with whatever rot had befallen the church—Doug, and Kirsty fell into chatting. Mike was nominally part of the conversation, but he had also been allowed to hold Toby, and most of his focus was on the infant's happy little face. He cooed, and spit bubbled in his tiny mouth as Mike rocked the child. He rarely regretted not having children. It had just never been a thing he wanted.

But when he held Toby—the little kid's beautiful eyes beaming up at him, the soft little nose, the wispy blond hair on his tiny head—sometimes he felt a tad bit of longing ... Either way, it was too late now. And he was perfectly happy to enjoy being a fun church uncle to Toby.

He just hoped neither of Toby's parents got sent to heaven soon.

Does Ted even know? Has he heard the rumors? Does he believe them? Does Kirsty tell him what goes on?

Mike pushed these thoughts out of his head and focused on Toby's smile.

Mike sat in one of the back pews, watching Reverend Victor's sermon. Every head in the congregation was locked firmly on the man behind the pulpit, holding raptly onto his every word. Not even a cough or the wrinkle of a hard candy wrapper interrupted the sermon. The church fell into a trance every time Reverend Victor spoke.

The pastor leaned against the pulpit as if resting his weight against it. He gripped the sides with white knuckles, spraying spit and salvation as he shouted.

Mike thought the sermon sounded very similar to all his previous ones: no substance, but plenty of passion. He spewed garbled nonsense with all the energy of a coked-up jack-rabbit, weaving from point to point with no discernible connection. One minute, he was talking about the sanctity of the blood of Jesus and the next, he was talking about how mosquitoes hadn't been allowed on Noah's Ark.

Reverend Victor's actions in the basement with Mike last Sunday had led him to believe that the reverend was *not* a God-fearing Christian. But he didn't even seem to have a good grasp on the religion he claimed. His sermons held all the biblical knowledge of a first grader with two Sunday school lessons under his belt.

They rarely held a central theme or idea, either. There was never a *point* the reverend wanted you to take home. It was just 45 minutes of rambling, followed by a ten-minute section at the end where the reverend would re-hash everything he'd told them about God blessing them with the closet and how lucky they were.

The congregation saw no faults in the sermons. Every sentence Reverend Victor spoke earned him nods and "mmm-hmms!" Any especially exciting points, usually a reference to the closet, got him a collection of rousing "Amens!" and "Yes Lord!"

The reverend slammed his hands on the pulpit as he hammered his point home. They were already in the section where he yammered on about the closet.

"Ohhh, church, what a *blessing* our good Lord has blessed us with. You folks have *earned* it. And it's gonna provide you with everything you have been seeking in your walk with the Lord. This is the last step! This is what you've been waiting for all your life!" Reverend Victor boomed.

Applause came from the more charismatic members of the congregation.

Watching Reverend Victor speak with the knowledge he now possessed made Mike's pits sweat. It felt like every goddamn thing under the sun made his pits sweat these days, but this time felt justified.

He hadn't known how the reverend would react to seeing him after their little "meeting," but the Reverend had acted like nothing happened. He'd strolled over to Mike with a big grin, stretching out the same hand he'd used to slap Mike across the face. Mike had shaken the reverend's hand with a sweaty palm and silently nodded as Reverend Victor chatted about football for a few moments. Mike felt a massive wave of relief once he moved on to other people.

The interaction disturbed him. How could he act so normal after what had happened in the basement? He knew he shouldn't be surprised based on the knowledge he now possessed. Reverend Victor had been lying to the congregation and sending them God knows where for months. Of course, he'd be a good liar.

"Oh, church ... our God is beautiful, isn't he?" Reverend Victor said.

"Amen!" the church responded.

Mike shifted in his seat. It was almost time for Reverend Victor to announce who would be the lucky person to get to go to heaven this week.

"Second Kings 2:11: And it came to pass, as they still went on, and talked, that, behold, there appeared a chariot of fire, and horses of fire, and parted them both asunder; and Elijah went up by a whirlwind into heaven," Reverend Victor said, referencing a Bible verse for the first time that Sunday.

"That's such a beautiful verse, isn't it church? It might be the best verse in the whole Bible. But today I've got a treat; I wanna read another one for ya ..." He thumbed through the pages of the Bible on the pulpit. The crackle of its paper thundered in the silent church.

The reverend cleared his throat. "Matthew 19:14: But Jesus said, Suffer little children, and forbid them not, to come unto me: for such is the kingdom of heaven."

The congregation remained silent. Mike raised an eyebrow, not sure what the reverend was getting at.

"Now folks ... some people try to keep our kids away from God, don't they? Yes, we all know someone who tried to impede our youngins having a good relationship with God." Reverend Victor turned his head, and his eyes locked firmly with Mike's. "And we must do whatever it takes to stop these people."

Mike swallowed, feeling targeted. He felt there was a message for him in the reverend's words. Something that would, paraphrased, be along the lines of: *don't fuck with anything I'm about to do.*

"But our Lord *wants* to see the children. He wants to love them! What's good for us is good for them, isn't it church?" Reverend Victor continued.

Mike paled. An inkling of an idea sprouted in his head, but ... the reverend wouldn't *dare,* would he? No. It was too far, even for him.

Reverend Victor peeled his lips back in his signature politician grin. He turned his beady eyes down toward Kirsty—who was rocking Toby.

"The Lord has informed me, in all his big, beautiful wisdom, that he wants to bring Toby home with him today," the reverend said.

Mike's heart leaped. His palms slicked with sweat. He waited for the boos to erupt. For the congregation to scream and shout that he'd finally gone too far. That Reverend Victor could send all the old fuddy duddys to heaven that he wanted, but an infant was too damn far.

Kirsty fell to her knees, her big, racking sobs booming through the church. But Mike wasn't mistaken for a second. They were tears of joy, not sadness. Her husband jumped up in the air, shouting and pumping his fists. The congregation erupted into cheers.

"No ... no no *no,*" Mike said. His words went unnoticed.

Reverend Victor beamed at the congregation. "Let's send this beautiful baby boy to heaven, folks!"

The congregation poured out of the pews—Kirsty and Toby bounded out first, heading straight toward the basement door with everyone else on their heels. Mike felt like everything was moving at double speed. He stumbled after them, panic building in his chest as he brought up the rear. This couldn't happen without the boy's *father* knowing!

"Folks, we can't ..." Mike said. But again, no one paid atten tion to him. They were too busy whooping and cheering and celebrating Toby's special day. Kirsty reached the basement first, jumping up and down with excitement. Toby bounced in her arms, a concerned frown on his little face.

How can she be so excited about losing her child?

Mike and the rest of the congregation filed into the basement. The congregation surged forward, crowding around the closet as close as they dared. Mike crept along the back wall, hoping that any minute he'd wake up in his bed, free of this nightmare.

The cheery expressions in front of him were the complete opposite of the ones he'd seen when Oakwood Baptist had attended the pro-life protest a couple of years back. Mike could vividly remember everyone's faces contorted into righteous fury as they fought back against the evils of abortion. Because they believed killing babies was wrong, didn't they?

Why did they celebrate when a baby would be sent to heaven now?

Sent to heaven—Christ—you know damn well heaven isn't behind that door.

Mike felt numb as he imagined whatever horrible fate had turned Rob into nothing but the aftermath of a castration befalling poor, innocent Toby. He couldn't let that happen. No, he *couldn't*. But God, how could he stop it?! Things were already moving along at breakneck speed.

He blinked, and Reverend Victor had Kirsty and Toby up in front of the closet. It was the same scene as last week and all the weeks before. Only now, there was no elation on the face of the person going to heaven. Toby's eyebrows furrowed, and his bottom lip was quivering as his blue eyes darted over all the people cheering at him. Mike's heart flipped in his chest. A ringing filled his ears.

The reverend spewed his usual bullshit. He quoted his verse. He gave a few words about the beauty of youth. And then the speed reversed, and everything fell into slow motion.

Mike watched as Kirsty reached the little bundle of blue blankets in her arms over to Reverend Victor. Toby's pudgy fists reached out to his mother as the reverend's ring-clad fingers wrapped around his body. The same fingers that had struck Mike across the face a week ago.

A whine escaped the boy's lips, reaching across the basement and twisting Mike's heart. The image of the fog, the memory of the scent, and the thought of the mangled penis spurred Mike into action. Whatever had happened to Rob, Tim, and all the others, it wouldn't happen to Toby.

Reverend Victor pulled open the closet door—

"Wait!" Mike barked.

The excited chatter died instantly. Every head snapped toward him; confused, glassy eyes regarded him. Reverend Victor turned to face Mike, raising an eyebrow. The piercing stare made Mike wilt. He wanted to run upstairs and hide under a pew. But he couldn't. Not with the child's life on the line.

Mike swallowed. He took a shaky breath. Goddamn, he wanted a cigarette.

"He ... isn't he too young?" Mike said.

Concerned murmurs rippled through the crowd.

"Too ... young?" Reverend Victor frowned.

Mike nodded. "He's only a baby."

Reverend Victor chuckled. "Didn't you hear the sermon, Mike? Jesus said suffer little children and forbid them *not* to come unto him."

Mike shifted from foot to foot. The weight of every eye on him made him want to fall to the floor. "Yes... but I think... doesn't that mean we should put him in Sunday school? It feels foolhardy to just take his life."

"Take his life?" Kirsty chuckled. "What do you mean by taking his life? He's gaining eternal life in heaven!"

"Amen!" Doug said, stamping his cane down.

"Praise GOD!" Mabel warbled.

Mike opened his mouth, but everything that he could say would be an indictment against the reverend, and he knew damn well no one would listen to that. Goddammit, he had to say *something!* Something that would postpone the ritual.

"But why would we separate the family? Shouldn't a child be with its mother as God intended?" Mike shouted, his voice going a pitch higher than normal. His panic was growing. Desperation flooded him. He was outnumbered. Everyone else in the room thought he was talking nonsense.

Reverend Victor closed his eyes and began murmuring. Prayers left his mouth and filled the room. The hushed congregation listened with bated breath. Mike's mind raced at the possibilities of what the reverend might say next.

Reverend Victor's eyes fluttered open. "Mike is right."

The congregation whispered to each other.

"Toby hasn't even stopped suckling from his mother's breast yet. God doesn't want to see them separated, does he church?" Reverend Victor said.

The congregation cheered and amened the same opinion that they had moments ago looked at with scorn. The only difference now was that Reverend Victor was the one professing it.

Mike turned to Kirsty, still holding the squirming little bundle that was Toby. "God has just told me he wants *both* of you to come to heaven!"

A deafening roar ripped through the room. Kirsty fell to her knees for the millionth time. Doug banged his cane against the walls and tried to get the church to chant, *"Hip, hip! Hooray!"*

"Mike, thank you for bringing that up! The Lord clearly placed it on your heart," Reverend Victor called across the sea of celebration between them. His mouth was pulled into a smile, but his eyes were hard and cold, carrying a simple message: *fuck nothing else up.*

Mike stumbled forward, walking toward the closet, but he couldn't cut through the people. Men grabbed his arms to celebrate. Women tried to reach up and kiss his cheek. Dancing old folks got in his way. Reverend Victor was snapping the closet door shut by the time he reached the front row.

He could charge the door. Rip Toby out and run far, far away from the church. But he didn't. Fear held him back. He knew he had to say something—*do* something. But he didn't. It was his word against the Reverend's. He had no proof.

He watched in horror as Reverend Victor slammed his palms into the closet door five times.

BAM! BAM! BAM! BAM! BAM!

The sound of prayer filled the room. Mike prayed silently.

God, please, please don't let it work this time. Save that beautiful baby boy and please don't let it happen to him.

God didn't listen. The lights flickered. Fog sprayed from the cracks in the door. The congregation whooped and cheered, dancing and kicking the smoke in the air. The stench tripled in the air, provoking a few hastily covered gags from the more elderly in the congregation. Mike's eyes watered both from the stench and the knowledge that something *horrible* was happening to Toby.

It seemed time had finally stopped. He remained suspended at that moment for an eternity. The death of an innocent infant and his mother happening just beyond that inch of wood. The congregation cheered around him. The acrid fog wrapped around him and seeped into his clothes.

And then Reverend Victor ripped the door open. The congregation cheered as the fog cleared and revealed that Kirsty and Toby were gone.

FIVE

MIKE SAT SLUMPED AT his kitchen table. The TV dinner he'd heated hours ago had gone cold, with nearly a dozen cigarette butts wrapped around it. The dim, yellow kitchen light hanging above Mike's head staved off the darkness of the night outside but did nothing for the festering blackness growing inside his chest.

He'd been the first to leave church. As soon as the closet door had been flung open, he'd stumbled back the way he came, not bothering to stick around for the usual celebration. He didn't think he could bear it. He'd driven home and plopped himself at the table, getting up only to piss, grab another pack of cigarettes, and heat his uneaten dinner.

You knew that closet was a trap, but you didn't stop it. You let that innocent baby get slaughtered.

He had tried to stop it. Damn it, he had! Nobody would listen to him. He had done everything he could.

But it wasn't good enough. They're dead now because of you.

Mike rubbed his forehead, biting down on another cigarette and lighting it up. God, he wanted to hold out hope. Part of him wanted to believe that even though the people weren't going to heaven, they might at least be kept alive. The thought of Rob's whacked-off cock strangled these hopes.

But does that mean the bodies are close by? Are they crammed in the walls somewhere? Is that why the church smells so fucking bad? Jesus Christ, why does Reverend Victor want this?

No answers to any of these questions, or any of the ones Mike had asked himself over the past nine hours, came to Mike's mind. But he knew one thing: it had to stop. No more people could get taken away. He would die before he let it happen again.

If they didn't want to believe him, that was fine. He would make them believe.

He pushed up from his kitchen chair, shuffling to his bedroom. He scrounged around under his bed, pushing aside dusty shoe boxes until he found what he was looking for. He pulled out a small black box, opening it, and finding a small, black camera. He clicked it open and confirmed there was still a roll of film inside.

Next, he raided the junk drawers. He had lost his only flashlight in the church during his last visit, and it was undoubtedly now with Rob's toupee. He found a two-pack of long candles. They would have to do.

He almost left with just those items, but halfway out the door, he paused. He stepped back into the kitchen, pulling a steak knife from the block on the counter. He tucked it inside his jacket pocket—intentionally avoiding any thoughts of what its purpose may be.

He dropped his keys twice as he tried to unlock his car. His hand felt like two useless bricks. His goddamn pits were sweaty again. He finally got into his car and slumped into the driver's seat.

He sat there for five minutes, not turning the car on, not shutting his door. Just sitting. Thinking about the monumental task he had set for himself.

He was out of his league here. There were forces at work here that he couldn't even comprehend. And he wanted nothing more than to get out of this car and run right up to his bed. Or better yet—slam the car door and peel out of Oakwood for good.

And then he thought of Toby, the picture of innocence, being mutilated in the same way that Rob had been.

Mike cranked the key in the ignition, and the car roared to life. He cranked gospel music and pulled out onto the road, gunning for Oakwood Baptist. The music was comforting, but it did nothing to drown out the worried thoughts racing through his mind. Reverend Victor would most likely be on high alert after Mike's first nighttime break-in. Reverend Victor would likely catch Mike again.

And what would happen to him if he was caught? Mike shuddered, thinking of the possibilities. The pictures that filled his mind made him itch to turn around. He would have, were it not for the child. Instead, he lit another cigarette. He was almost sick of the things. His fingers were yellowed with tar. The stale scent hung thicker on his clothes than it ever had. But God, he needed some comfort now more than ever.

Two cigarettes later, Oakwood Baptist crested into view. He slowed quickly, cutting his headlights. Squinting through the windshield, he gleaned that the parsonage lights were off. That brought him a modicum of comfort, but he still pulled the car to the side of the road, parking under the cover of the trees.

He slipped out and locked the doors, then began the trek up to the church. Every time he dared to glance at the parsonage, he imagined the reverend slamming the screen door open and charging at him. His fears never materialized, though, and after a moment of walking, he reached the church.

Another glance told him that there was still no sign of life from the parsonage. Not even a sly finger peeling down a single-blind from the window to reveal a probing eye.

Mike hurried up the steps and pushed against the door. It didn't give. Locked.

Damn it.

That confirmed Mike's suspicions that Reverend Victor *was* being more cautious this time around.

Just go home, a little voice in the back of his head told him. Mike desperately wanted to listen to it. But he couldn't. He had to get proof.

Mike slunk around the side of the church. He had to squint in the pale moonlight and run his fingers along the rough side of the church just to have a sense of direction. He kept his ears open, half expecting to hear the reverend's southern voice behind him at any moment. The voice never came, and the only thing he heard was the swish of his shoes in the grass and the light whistle of the wind.

He stopped when he felt the side door that led into the sanctuary. He tried the handle. It rattled, but didn't give. Also locked. Mike huffed and continued around to the back of the church. The only other door was the side door he'd just tried, but he had one more hope.

The window to Reverend Victor's office was right at chest level. Its blinds were drawn—had been ever since Reverend Victor had taken over—but maybe ...

Mike stepped up to it, pushing his hands under the lip. The window popped open an inch. Relief flooded through him. He opened the window to a Mike-sized hole and hoisted himself up. He immediately felt his age, hissing as his joints and achy muscles yelled at him from the exertion. His shin, still sore from bashing into the pew a week ago, banged against the wall painfully. He made more noise than he should've as he clattered with the blinds and tipped over into the office, landing on the floor with a wheezy "Goddammit to hell."

After laying on the floor for a moment to catch his breath, Mike hoisted himself to his feet, groaning the whole way up. He shut the window he'd come from and resisted the urge to turn on a light. He doubted Reverend Victor would notice the light in his office was on, but he still pulled out a candle and lit it with his cigarette lighter.

Warm light filled the room, dancing off an enormous oak desk and three empty bookshelves. Reverend Joe Mitchell had kept the shelves filled with many Biblical books. Bibles mainly, but also Greek and Hebrew translation books, sets of commentaries, and some devotionals. Reverend Victor kept the shelves bare.

Mike crept out of the office and into the sanctuary. The wood under the red carpet creaked and groaned as he moved. He crossed in front of the stage and came to a stop in front of the basement door. The flame of the candle trembled in his shaking hands.

He suddenly felt foolish for plunging downstairs all by himself. But who could he have brought? Who would willingly sneak under Reverend Victor's nose? He was in this thing alone, whether he liked it or not. He swallowed the lump in his throat.

"For Toby."

Mike pushed open the door, its familiar creak grating against his ears. The candlelight did next to nothing against the deep black of the steps. Going downstairs became an impossible task in his mind. His heartbeat thundered in his chest; his mouth dried.

I can't do it. I can't do it, I can't do it, I can't do it.

Toby's sweet little face came to his mind, smiling and giggling. Unaware of the horrors it would die to. The horrors that Mike hadn't even seen yet. The horrors the congregation didn't know existed.

Mike sucked in a breath. "Yea, though I walk through the valley of the shadow of death, I will fear no evil: for thou art with me; thy rod and thy staff comfort me."

The verse was swallowed up by the dark mouth that was the staircase. But it made Mike feel brave enough to plunk his first foot down. The step creaked. The stench danced in his nose. He forced his other foot to follow its brother. He repeated the verse in his mind, chanting it over and over until the words lost meaning and sounded like gibberish.

One foot after the other, he crept down the steps until he emerged into the basement. The candlelight danced on the walls, not chasing away the darkness but intertwining with it, orange and black dancing together. The air in the basement felt thicker than it did on the stairs, as if he were wading in syrup. Gooseflesh rippled up his back and arms. His insides twisted.

I'm not alone.

The thought came to him, not as a hasty, fearful jolt, but as a simple matter of fact. He groped on the wall for the light switch. The lights flicked on with a *buzz*. He scanned the room with frenzied eyes, but saw no one else. The basement was empty, sans its usual folding tables and leftover coffee cups.

The closet stared at him from the other side of the room. He swallowed, pacing toward it with slow, intentional steps.

That's where Toby went. That's where Toby went to die.

He set his candle, still lit, on the table closest to the closet and pulled the camera out of his jacket pocket. He stood there for a few minutes, stalling the inevitable, but unable to move forward.

Get it over with, damn it, he scolded himself.

He scurried up to the closet and banged a fist against it five times.

Bam! Bam! Bam! Bam! Bam!

He twisted the knob and jerked the door open, scurrying back a good ten feet away. He itched to run farther, gluing himself to the opposite wall, but he knew the photos had to be undeniable. He readied the camera and jammed his thumb on the button. The flashbulb popped; the shutter clicked.

There was his establishing picture. Proof that it was the closet he was taking pictures of. Now he just needed pictures of what happened next ...

His heart hammered. His breaths came in shallow gasps.

The lights cut, plunging him into candlelight. They didn't flicker as they usually did, they just disappeared.

HISSSSssssssssss...

Fog began coasting out of the closet. Mike brought his shirt over his nose and breathed through his mouth. Even with those precautions, his eyes watered from the sulfuric stench. He bottled up a cough, begging to be released, and snapped another picture. The flash lit up the basement in perfect white light for a split second.

Crrrrreaaaaaak.

The wood in the closet groaned. Mike gripped the camera as tight as he could to keep his hands from shaking. He mashed the shutter button, and another flash of light filled the room. Clouds of fog, the shelves in the closet, the white folding tables, and the wood-paneled walls were all lit up barely long enough to see them before the flash disappeared and left the room to be lit by a puny candle.

Mike retched. The stench was seeping through his shirt, overwhelming him with nausea. He hastily wiped away his tears with his sleeves.

Crrrrreaaaaaaaak.

Mike readied the camera and snapped another picture. White light from the flash blasted the room. And there—in the closet—he saw it. Gone as quickly as it came, but there. A shadow. Moving near the top of the closet.

Shaped like an arm.

Mike felt like pissing his pants. His pits were sweating like the goddamn fountain of youth. His eyes were bulging out of his skull, straining in the candlelight, trying to see what the flash had briefly lit up.

There! There's your proof! Get out now!

Mike gagged. The stench worsened. Tears and snot streamed down his face in a steady flow. He knew he couldn't go back yet. The congregation wouldn't turn their backs on Reverend Victor based on a grainy photo of a vague, arm-shaped thing. They'd just say it was God's arm.

Mike needed more.

He snatched the candle from the table, stretching it out in front of him. Its dim orange glow pulsed on the frame of the closet door, but he was still too far away for the light to reach inside.

He inched toward the gaping black maw, camera, and candle both held out in front of him as if they could ward away whatever evil waited inside. More fog coughed toward him. It reached up to his thighs now.

The stench worsened with every step he took. It enveloped him, assaulting every one of his senses. He could taste it thick on his tongue; he could feel it plunging deep into his nose; he could feel the acidity of it on his skin.

An overwhelming sense of dread took him, flushing through his body. His legs locked. The closet was dimly lit by the candle now. He could see the dark outlines of the shelves.

And then two things happened at once.

Mike smashed the shutter button—the flashbulb popped and lit up the room at the same time as *it* dropped from above the top of the closet frame. Mike screamed at the movement, not yet comprehending what he was seeing. And then the candlelight crept around the shape, illuminating a sight that Mike would see in his dreams every night for the rest of his life.

Toby, the baby Reverend Victor had so easily discarded, dangled from the top of the closet, his arms strung above him. The dead child's body flopped around as it dangled. His head bobbed on his shoulders, pitching forward to reveal a crater in the top of his skull the size of a pool ball. His brains had been reduced to mush. They sloshed around and dripped down the front of his bloodied, bruised face.

Mike dropped the camera. It clattered to the ground. His hand shook, making the candlelight jitter over the dead infant hanging in front of him. He wanted to scream, cry, and vomit, but all he could do was stand bolted to the floor and stare at the repulsive, *vile* sight in front of him.

Two bones protruded from Toby's gored calves where his feet had been gnawed off. Tendons, veins, and muscles flapped off the end of his legs, slapping against each other like lunch meat and sending blood dripping to the floor. Most of the skin on his body had been ripped off to varying extents. Some wounds were deeper than others, exposing bone and organs, while some looked as if sandpaper had been taken to his skin.

The corpse flapped and jiggled, and Mike realized that the motion hadn't just been from the movement of falling, that the child was being jostled around. A bit of skin slipped off of Toby's arm and landed on the ground with a splat.

He wasn't just being jostled. He was being made to look like he was dancing, puppetted like a marionette. Mike's stomach twisted at the mean-spiritedness of the act. And at the realization that someone or something was intentionally doing it.

Heart thumped against his rib cage, bile welled in the back of Mike's throat and tears streamed down his cheeks. He wanted to run miles away from the church and gouge his eyes out. But he knew the only way to stop this was for everyone else to see. For the congregation to reckon with the truth of what was really happening in the closet.

He stooped into the fog and retrieved his camera, bringing the device up to his blotchy eyes and snapping another photo. The white light filled the room, bringing the dead, dancing baby into nauseating clarity but also illuminating something else ...

Two hands protruding from behind the top of the door frame wrapped firmly around Toby's bloodied arms. If they could even be called hands. Something was wrong with them, Mike could tell, even though he'd only seen them for a fraction of a second. He let out a sharp gasp and mashed the shutter button once more. The flash lit up the hands again.

They were long. Spindly and gray, the fingers wrapped around Toby's arms fully two times, coiling like string. No fingernails adorned the tips, making the sickly flesh look rubbery. Despite the lack of nails, they still dug into Toby's arms, the baby's blood welling around them.

There was something alive in the closet. Something was killing them. Whether for food or sport, Mike didn't know, nor did he care. All that he needed to know was apparent: the thing had killed a child, and it found it fit to play with the child as if it were a doll.

It was teasing him, mocking him. It *knew* that Mike found the sight abhorrent, and it was doing it for the sole purpose of causing Mike turmoil.

Mike stumbled backward. The candlelight retracted with each of his footsteps, slowly allowing darkness to creep around the edges of the dancing child and then envelop it completely. Mike continued shuffling backward, his whole body rigid as if his veins had been pumped with concrete.

He had his pictures. He had his proof. And now everyone would have to listen. They would *have* to.

The closet succumbed to the darkness fully as the last flicker of candlelight within the distance licked the stump of Toby's leg. The only thing Mike faced now was a dark void. But he could still hear the wet, meaty slaps of the child.

And then it stopped.

Mike froze. A voice in the back of his head screamed at him to keep going, to get out now. But part of him worried about the sudden silence. What if the arms had emerged from the closet? What if he had to distract it or throw something at it? God in heaven, what did the rest of it look like?

Toby soared toward him, the child's limbs bent and broken, one eye dangling out of its socket, blood and brains spraying behind it like a comet trail.

Six

Toby's sailing corpse hit Mike square in the chest, crushing the air out of his lungs and sending him flying. Toby exploded on impact, splashing an all-encompassing monsoon of blood around Mike, extinguishing the candle in a wave of red. Bone and flesh smeared across his body, spraying up into his face, nose, and mouth with the force of a firehose. The metallic taste of infant blood provoked a stream of vomit from his stomach. It gushed over his lips, dribbling down his chin and melding with the gore that covered him.

He slammed into the ground, his spine jabbing against the unyielding carpet. His chest burned, his muscles aching, his lungs screaming for air. He gasped for a breath, aspirating drops of blood and a bit of Toby's left ear. He vomited again, forcing himself to roll on his side and spew the liquid.

BRRROOOMMMMPH!

He slammed his blood-soaked hands against his ears. A tooth-rattling trumpet boomed through the basement. It sounded like an eager and malicious elephant.

Pain echoed through his trembling body. His mind struggled to grapple with the depravity of Toby's fate. He could hear the baby's destroyed body squelching under him. Muscle and sinew, not even a year old, slipped off his chest as he sucked in a rattled breath. He was aware of the fact that his mind was breaking at that moment, unable to process the depravity it had just experienced. His vision blurred. Numbness spread from his head to the rest of him. His facial expression slackened. A shrill ringing filled his ears, compounding with the elephant's roar.

BRRRROOOMMMMMPH!... eeeeeeeeeeeeeeeee...

He wanted to lie down, be still, and ignore the dripping guts that coated every inch of his body.

Thump ... thump ... thump ...

The thing was emerging from the closet. He could feel its slow, methodical footsteps reverberating through the ground underneath him. He ignored the urge to lie down and scrambled to his feet, slipping in the blood, guts, and vomit under him. His shoes squelched over a tiny line of intestines, and he fell to the ground again. His teeth slammed together, sending stars shooting through his head. He wanted to curl up in a ball and remain as still as possible so the body matter beneath him would finally stop making noise. He would stay that way forever. Until he died or went insane, he didn't care. He already felt halfway to insane.

Thump ... thump ... thump ...

The footsteps boomed closer, rattling him. His body did not care that his mind wanted to lie here. It had one priority: survive.

He slipped up to all fours, his palms mashing baby muscle into the carpet. He dragged himself to the foot of the stairs, grabbing them with his hands and pulling himself to his knees, then his feet. He hurled himself up the stairs, trailing goo like a snail. His shoes slipped several times, but he kept running up the stairs.

BRRRROOOMMMMMPH!

The sound hammered against his eardrums. He threw himself into the sanctuary, stumbling forward into a pew, slumping into it. He gasped deep breaths of air and spat a gob of Toby's blood to the floor.

BRRRROOOMMMMPH!

The sound rattled the walls of the church. Mike yanked himself up from the pew and gunned toward the front door. He didn't give a shit if Reverend Victor saw him now. Once he got those pictures developed, Reverend Victor was—*God fucking cock sucking, damn it!!!*

He froze, clenching his teeth. He'd dropped the camera when Toby had exploded on him.

Just leave, a voice in the back of his head begged him. He wanted to obey it. But if he did, then everything he'd experienced here would be for nothing. He'd be right back where he started—watching poor, oblivious souls get sucked up to the same fate that Toby had met.

Mike whimpered. He let the doorknob slip from his hands and stumbled back down the aisle of pews. He couldn't leave without the camera, but he also couldn't go back into that basement. It was a death sentence. He needed reinforcements.

He shambled into the reverend's office, still dripping copious amounts of blood that wasn't his.

How much blood is inside a baby? He thought numbly as he slammed the door and twisted the lock. For good measure, he dragged the chair facing the reverend's desk over and propped it under the handle.

He clicked on the lamp as he sat behind the desk. He found it difficult to worry that Reverend Victor might see the light after what he'd just experienced.

An unexpected sob barked out from his throat. He covered his mouth and scrunched up his eyes, willing the tears to remain in their ducts.

What just happened? What did I see down there?

He felt as if he'd been granted a glimpse of hell itself. Pure, unfettered evil.

He peeled his face from his hands, sticky blood peeling, and grabbed the phone. He dialed 911, leaving red marks on the rotary numbers. After three rings, a woman's voice responded.

"911, what's your emergency?"

Mike took a deep, shuddery breath. "I'm at Oakwood Baptist Church. A child has been killed."

"How old is the child?"

"An infant," Mike said. He fumbled in his damp pockets and retrieved a cigarette, lighting it up and sucking in the smoke.

"When did this happen?"

Mike trembled. He could feel his resolve slipping, and he worried that once he broke down, he would be inconsolable and completely useless.

"Please, just send someone," he said.

"Police are on the way. You said the child is dead? Are they responsive at all? Has anyone tried CPR?"

A shrill laugh shot past Mike's lips. CPR? On the bloody pulp of a mess smeared across the carpet downstairs?

The woman was talking some more, but Mike couldn't hear her that well. The only things he could hear were the sound the child's body had made when it was puppet into its cruel dance, the sound of Toby exploding against his chest, the sound of himself wallowing in its gore, the sound of its blood squeaking under his shoes as he fled that... *thing*.

That thing which was still in the church with him.

Fear roiled in Mike's stomach. He stood from the chair, feeling ancy, like an animal in a trap. The phone clattered to the desk, the operator's continued droning forgotten.

He couldn't bear being in the same building as that thing. Any moment, he expected it to appear in the dimly lit office, grotesquely long fingers reaching out for him. But he couldn't bring himself to unlock the door to the sanctuary.

So he waited in the office, pacing the room. The only thing that kept him sane was the mantra he repeated in his mind.

Get the camera so the others can see. That's the only way this all stops.

He worried the creature would destroy the camera and all the photos. But part of him knew it wouldn't. The camera was a small, black device in a sea of gore and fog in the dark basement. It probably hadn't even noticed it.

He knew this hope was only a coping mechanism, and it was 50/50 whether the camera would be there when the police descended those steps into hell, but he held onto it as tight as he could.

After what felt like a hundred years, he heard the faint sounds of police sirens growing louder.

He ripped the chair out from under the handle and threw the door open. He sprinted through the sanctuary, miraculously not colliding with any pews and bursting through the double doors to the church. Red and blue lights glowed on the grassy lawn of the church as a cop car rumbled into the parking lot.

Mike fell to his knees. Tears of relief slid down his face.

Two cops emerged from the cruiser, hands in their holsters. One was a tall man with a bald head, and the other a dark-haired woman.

"What's going on?" the man asked.

"We have to get the camera. It's the only way they'll believe me," Mike said.

The cops shot each other a look and then regarded Mike again.

"Where's the child?" the woman said.

All over me.

"Downstairs," Mike said

The dark-haired cop shuffled up to her partner, murmuring in his ear. "This is the church with the rumors."

"Don't believe them," Mike said. "He can't send people to heaven. It's a lie. It's something else. It's something *horrible.*"

The cops shared another look. The woman stepped up to Mike.

"What's your name, sir?"

"Mike."

"Alright, Mike, you look like you're not doing too good. You wanna come sit in the back of my car and warm up?"

Mike nodded. The blood all over his body was drying. It cracked on his skin. He let the woman lead him away from the church and to the cop car. The bright lights gave him a headache. She opened the door for him, and Mike slumped inside—letting the warmth envelop him like a hug.

"Sit tight," the cop said before shutting the door.

Mike leaned his head back against the headrest. He closed his eyes, but the second he did, images of what he'd just experienced filled his mind. He snapped them open, turning to watch the church instead. It was better than seeing that scene again.

Mike choked back a sob. He was inches away from breaking down, barely able to keep the gravity of what had just happened from crashing down on him.

Hold on a little longer. They have to see. They have to see the truth.

Mike watched the still church building. The police had turned on the lights when they'd gone in. The stained glass windows glowed from the inside out, but it didn't look any less scary. The building was permanently ruined in his mind. Once Reverend Victor had been fired, thrown in prison—or hell, given the electric chair—Mike was going to demand that the elders move the congregation, and the building they currently occupied be burned down.

And let that thing down there burn to a crisp.

Mike swallowed. Did it live in the closet? Or was this like some kooky sci-fi novel, and there was a dimension it was from, and it only transported to the closet when you tapped on the door five times? Mike shuddered, thinking of its pale, spindly fingers—how those fingers would feel running down his body.

The image of the hands dangling the infant came back in his mind. He cringed and rapped his head on the window, trying to dislodge the vision from his mind.

"Please, God, take that sight from me," Mike moaned.

Mike didn't even want to consider the implications these events could have on his belief in God. With the church completely in Reverend Victor's grip, his faith was all he had left.

He kept his eyes peeled, still watching the church, trying not to even let himself blink, lest his mind show him that cursed vision for even a split second. He didn't know how long he sat there. It could have been five minutes. It could have been five hours.

BANG!

He jumped in his seat. The sharp crack of a gunshot boomed from the church.

His breathing quickened. Had the cops met the creature in the closet? Was it dead? Hope filled Mike's chest. Was it possible that this nightmare was over?

He waited. The green, glowing numbers on the dashboard's clock passed by, but the cops still didn't emerge from the church. Mike tried the door handle, but it didn't give.

The lights of the church went out. A second later, the double doors swung open.

Reverend Victor strolled out.

Cold dread poured into Mike's stomach like ice water. "No. No, no, no."

Reverend Victor strolled down the steps. His white suit billowed in the summer wind. His face was stoic. Locked in on the cop car Mike sat in.

"NO! GOD WHY!" Mike roared. He threw himself backward against the door, fumbling with the latch. It didn't open. He tried the other. It didn't open.

He rammed his fingers against the mesh separating the back from the front—damning the cop in his mind for trapping him in the back.

Reverend Victor marched closer.

Mike brought his legs up and kicked at the partition as hard as he could. It only sent more pain up his sore legs.

These keep hardened criminals locked in the back; there's no way you'd be able to kick it down, he thought deliriously.

He kept trying. It was his only hope. He frantically slammed his feet into it over and over. The car shook and jostled, and his legs screamed in pain, but the partition remained rock solid.

Reverend Victor's face lit up in the glow of the flashing lights. He glared through the window at Mike, then ripped open the door.

"Get out," Reverend Victor hissed.

Mike was frozen, cowering on the other side of the car from the pastor. Reverend Victor growled and lunged in, grabbing Mike's ankle and yanking.

"HELP! HELP OH GOD!" Mike squealed.

Reverend Victor dragged him out of the car, dropping him onto the asphalt of the parking lot. He slammed the door, then crouched down until his face was a foot away from Mike's.

"You're becoming a real pain in the ass, Mike. You know that?" he growled.

Mike blubbered underneath the man. Snot dripped from his nose, and tears welled in his eyes, dampening the dried blood on his face.

"P-p-please don't put me in the closet," Mike said.

Reverend Victor shook his head, glancing back at the church. "Goddamn, Mike, you don't know how badly I want to. I just sent those two cops to heaven."

Mike's stomach turned. He'd condemned those innocent people to the same fate as Toby.

"What in God's name is down there?"

A grin split Reverend Victor's face. "Oh, you didn't see?"

"I saw two hands. Two *demonic* hands," Mike spat. A bit of rage bubbled up within him. Reverend Victor caused all the horrible things that had happened to Mike. He was the person who had brought whatever that *thing* was to the church.

Reverend Victor leaned even closer, smiling widely. The smell of expensive cologne washed over Mike.

"You don't think I'm sending those people to heaven, do you?" he asked.

"No."

"And who's gonna believe you?" Reverend Victor said.

Mike didn't answer.

"Count yourself lucky, Mike. I can't send you to heaven yet ..."

Reverend Victor dug into his pocket, pulling out Mike's camera. Any faint bit of hope that Mike had kept through all the horrible events that had transpired vanished as Reverend Victor popped out the film canister.

He threw the camera over his shoulders. It shattered against the concrete—plastic, and glass skidded in all directions.

Reverend Victor chuckled, looking down at the cartridge. "You don't know people like I do, Mike... you think something like this would matter to them?"

He tossed it down, stopping on it and grinding it to the ground with a horrible, plasticky *crunch*.

"No," Mike said, watching the proof he'd held moments ago suddenly cease to exist. His heart broke. Despair welled in him like a clogged toilet.

Reverend Victor shook his head. "Mike, I would send you to heaven, but you made an awful mess in that basement. And *I'm* sure as hell not gonna be the one to clean it up."

Seven

Mike lay flat on the bed, staring up at the dark ceiling of Reverend Victor's guest bedroom. His wrists were bound tightly with duct tape, as were his ankles. The smell of Toby's blood was still thick in his nose, but the stench of the church wasn't noticeable in the parsonage.

Reverend Victor had tied him up, then dragged him to the parsonage, dropping him on the guest bed. He'd scolded Mike like a dog prone to shitting in the house and told him not to try escaping. Then he'd left. Mike had seen through the window as the reverend drove off with the police car. He returned half an hour later, walking down the street whistling, no sign of the car.

He'd slithered back into the house, whistling a gospel song and stopping in the doorway to the bedroom. The light from the house backlit him, making his face a dark shadow as he talked to Mike.

"Tomorrow, you're gonna clean up that big mess you made in the basement," Reverend Victor drawled. Mike's stomach churned at the idea of going back down into that hellish place. The realization that he'd have to see—*touch*—what was left of Toby made him silently cry again.

"And then you're gonna spend the week here with me. I can't be having you run off and cause trouble for me every night," Reverend Victor grumbled, as if Mike had caused him a grave inconvenience.

"After this week ... I'm going to send you to heaven. You'll celebrate like the rest of the church expects you to, and then ... well, that's that."

"Let me go," Mike choked.

Reverend Victor barked a laugh, then pulled the door shut, plunging Mike into darkness. Not that he minded. Darkness removed the sight of his bloodstained clothes. A second later, he heard the TV in the living room turn on.

Mike rolled to his side, wincing at the dozen places his body hurt. The restraints on his arms and legs dug into his skin, but he found it harder and harder to care about the pain. Everything hurt. Inside and out.

Reverend Victor was going to send him to heaven. Whatever was in that closet was going to kill him. That thought should've made Mike panic. His mind should be racing right now—trying to figure out how he was going to survive.

But... he almost didn't want to, though. Death, in some ways, seemed the preferable option. He couldn't imagine himself ever living life again after what he'd experienced in the church's basement. Contrary to making him panic, the idea that this nightmare would be over in a week brought him comfort. If only Reverend Victor had put him in that damn closet and gotten things over with tonight.

"I'm sorry, Lord," Mike mumbled, not sure for what exactly he was apologizing. Suppose he got killed in that closet, which seemed the only likely outcome. That would mean he would go to heaven, wouldn't it? So, in a roundabout way, Reverend Victor would send him to heaven, he supposed.

If he'd made it in.

Mike closed his eyes. His brain began replaying the scene from hours ago, making him relive the horror over and over again.

Cleaning the church went worse than Mike thought.

He followed Reverend Victor down the basement stairs, cringing at the stench. He'd been trying to mentally prepare himself for what he was going to see all morning, but as soon as he caught sight of the aftermath of his encounter with the thing in the closet, he buckled. His knees hit the floor. His stomach gurgled.

"I'm gonna be sick," he said, clutching his hands to his gut.

"Goddamn you, is all you do vomit?" Reverend Victor spat. "If you're sick, do it in the toilet."

Mike swallowed, forcing away the nausea as best he could.

It was even worse in the harsh, bright overhead lights. Guts and blood were ground deep into the carpet from where Mike had stumbled and fled. Most of the infant was destroyed beyond recognition. Reduced to a blackening, red smear. But there were little bits that held their shape enough to make Mike's heart twist painfully.

A small kneecap. A bit of scalp. An eye. A nose.

Reverend Victor stood on the last step, sneering at the gore like it was gross as dog shit, but nothing more disturbing.

"Well. Get to work," Reverend Victor said.

He smoked as Mike cleaned up, careful to keep his white suit clean and his brown loafers off of anything gross. The reverend had taken the duct tape off Mike's limbs, with the clear caveat that should Mike try to escape, he would be killed immediately.

Mike had to bag up all the solid pieces first. He ended up puking several times—running to the small, rickety basement bathroom and heaving his guts into the dusty toilet until there was nothing left inside of him. Only after the fourth trip to the bathroom, where he'd gotten up nothing more than clear bile, was he able to really begin the work.

Closing his eyes and fumbling around with his gloved hands, he loaded all the solid chunks into a large trash bag, which he took out to the dumpster under Reverend Victor's watchful eye.

Next, he scrubbed the carpets. The harsh, chemical smell of cleaner filled his nose, and chased away the thick, acrid stench of blood. Reverend Victor propped up a fan at the back of the room, pointing it toward the stairs.

"Gotta get that *stink* out," he grumbled.

Mike thought it was rich that Reverend Victor was bothered by the smell of the infant's corpse, but not that the church constantly smelled like a rotten egg. He felt a pang of hatred at the man for his callousness. Could he not show a shred of respect for Toby even in death?

Mike spent an hour scrubbing. His arms ached. Two hours later, they burned. Four hours total, and his arms felt as if they'd fallen off. It didn't matter how much he rotated or what method he used; his arms were constantly alight with pain and fatigue.

By the time Mike finished the carpet, the sun had set, and night had fallen completely. Mike scrubbed himself in the bathroom—taking advantage of the opportunity to wash his face, hands, and arms of the dried gore that was still on him from the previous night.

Reverend Victor saw what he was doing and dragged him out of the bathroom.

"I didn't tell you to take a shower," he scoffed. "Now look, you got bloody water all over the bathroom floor, dammit!"

"Can I please just change my clothes?" Mike begged.

Reverend Victor wrapped fresh rounds of tape around Mike's wrists.

"You could've changed your clothes all you want. You could've changed your clothes a hundred times a day if you'd just minded your damn business and not bothered me so much. No, I think you need to experience the consequences of your actions." He grabbed Mike's arm and marched him back to the parsonage.

He threw Mike back into the guest room. About half an hour later, Reverend Victor returned and tossed a fast-food cheeseburger and a bottle of water to the floor beside Mike's mattress. The sun had set while he was gone, but he still didn't turn on the light in the bedroom.

Mike rolled over and took the water bottle. It was tricky opening it with both of his hands knotted together, but he got the cap off. He chugged down all 16 ounces greedily, then dropped the bottle back to the floor. It clunked hollowly.

The familiar hum of Reverend Victor's TV came muffled through the wall. Mike lay flat on the mattress, the water sloshing uncomfortably in his stomach. He was starving, but he didn't much feel like eating. Cleaning the aftermath of Toby's desecration had done nothing to invigorate his will to live. Seeing his own hands slowly but surely wipe and scrub away any evidence of what had happened broke down his spirit.

But he supposed in six days, it would all be over.

The image that Mike had in his head for the man he knew as Reverend Victor crumbled in the week that he spent with him. Though Mike spent most of his time counting the lines on the wood-paneled walls surrounding him, sometimes he was allowed out to go to the bathroom. Or to the sink for water.

During these times, he got to see the real side of the pastor.

Reverend Victor had appeared as a smooth, suave, fancy man. Always flaunting his watches and designer suits and riding around town in his shiny car. And boy, did he have the charisma to back up this lavish lifestyle. He had a way of talking to you that made you feel you were the only person in the room.

That Reverend Victor, Mike learned, was a character.

Reverend Victor privately was not fancy or polished. The second he stepped over the threshold of his parsonage and no longer had to put on a show for the members of the congregation, everything changed.

For one, Reverend Victor ate nothing but fast food. Mike knew the man was wealthy—that was clear no matter what—but every day for lunch and dinner, Reverend Victor drove into town and came back with white, grease-stained bags filled with burgers, fries, chicken tenders, milkshakes, and other cheap artery-clogging goodies.

He'd toss Mike a handful of fries or a few chicken tenders and then plop himself in the recliner behind the TV. Reverend Victor spent most of his time watching the television. He watched home shopping channels, ketchup-slathered hand hovering above the telephone so he could call in whenever something caught his eye.

Every day, he got multiple packages. Stuff from the home shopping channels, stuff from magazines, stuff he'd had specially made and ordered. Watches, clothes, cassettes, VHS tapes, porno magazines, porno *films,* and a million other things showed up on the porch.

Reverend Victor was wealthy—how? Mike didn't know. God knows the measly offering from Oakwood Baptist wouldn't fund this level of shopping addiction. Maybe he came from family money?

Mike quickly dismissed that idea. Reverend Victor might be insanely rich, but he had absolutely no class. He ate like a child, swore like a sailor, and collected as many ugly, gaudy goods as his grubby little fists could reach for. If anyone who came from family money saw what Reverend Victor spent his money on, they'd have a heart attack.

Mike didn't know why he spent so much time thinking about it. He laughed at Reverend Victor once as a glob of mustard slipped off his hot dog and plopped on his white suit right as he was lecturing a woman on the home shopping channel for sending him the wrong chambray work shirt.

Mike stopped himself as the smile crept on his face.

That man is going to kill you. And all of your friends are going to cheer and thank him as he does it.

After that thought, it didn't seem so funny anymore.

The only time Mike saw the reverend slip back into his stage persona was when he had a woman over. He'd cram all of his recent purchases into the spare bedroom with Mike and tidy the house. He'd put on a clean suit, brush his teeth, and then be back to the old Reverend Victor that Mike recognized.

It surprised Mike how many women Reverend Victor saw. They were all from the church—some newer, but many were members who'd been attending for years. Women who Mike had been friends with for years. Women who Mike knew had husbands.

Every other night, a woman came knocking on the door. During these visits, Mike was instructed to stay in his room, even if it meant shitting himself and to not make a peep.

Tonight was no different. He lay on his mattress, listening as Reverend Victor's bed squeaked and squeaked, and Myrtle, who had been on Mike's mail route when he was working, moaned and hollered.

What in God's name do they see in him? He thought incredulously. *He's old, wrinkled, and sloppy.*

Mike knew if any of those women could see how Reverend Victor acted when he was alone, they wouldn't be so eager to get in his pants then.

The thought brought Mike some satisfaction, but then he realized ... that they *wouldn't* care. He strained his brain, trying to think of *any* scenario in which the congregation could be convinced that there was anything negative about the reverend.

Maybe it was just his newfound nihilism, but he couldn't think of one.

A burning hatred rushed into his stomach. It was the strongest emotion he'd felt since the disgust he'd suffered when he'd been forced to clean up the remains of Toby from the basement.

He hated Reverend Victor. He hated the man so much. The stupid pastor was the reason for all the horrible things that had happened to Mike. *He'd* brought that thing in there. *He'd* been the one to lead good Christian folk to their deaths. *He'd* been the one who made Mike spend a week covered in the same clothes an infant had exploded upon.

Maybe Mike could've stomached it all if it had been the actions of a smooth, cunning agent of Satan who could fast-talk even the wisest Christian.

But Reverend Victor was none of that! He was a greasy loser who liked to pretend he was hot stuff, screwing the wives of the men he was supposed to pastor. But he was still an old man, eating horrible food and yelling at the TV, even if he acted like he was the second coming of Jesus.

But everyone saw him for who he portrayed himself as. They'd fallen for it hook, line, and sinker. Well, Mike hadn't. And a lot of good it had done him.

Mike wondered if the church had been hypnotized. Forced into all of this. That would explain their glassy eyes and infallible perception of the reverend. But why? And *how?*

And damn it, why didn't it work on me?

Myrtle howled and moaned some more. Reverend Victor grunted. The bed underneath them squeaked and squeaked.

Mike's hatred for the pastor grew with every thrust.

The days ticked down. Sunday grew closer. The two constants in Mike's life became his growing acceptance of his impending death and his pure hatred for the man holding him hostage.

Nightmares plagued him. They forced him to relive that night in the basement in vivid detail, often incorporating other elements.

The worst one came Saturday night. He was standing in front of the closet, only this time, all the lights were on, so he saw in startling clarity *exactly* how the baby had exploded across his chest.

In the dream, he fell to his knees and began gathering up the blood and guts as if he could put it back together again. And then the whole church was there, surrounding him. And they were furious at him. They held him responsible for it. They glared down at him with furious eyes as he scrambled around in the baby soup.

"I didn't do it! There's something in the closet! Go look for yourselves!" he screamed.

They didn't listen. They just turned around. Reverend Victor was there with them now, smiling and chuckling like he didn't have blood on his hands. The congregation lined up in front of him. One by one, they kneeled before him and gave him oral sex. Men and women both sucked on his penis until he orgasmed thick streams of blood. Mike knew they would expect him to do the same. He was in the back of the line, but it was moving quickly.

Mike woke up with a start. He'd soaked through his clothes with sweat. Between the gore from a week ago and a week's worth of sweat and no showers, Mike smelled putrid. He'd grown used to it, but whenever he slept and woke up, his nose reset. The stench hit him full force as he blinked his groggy eyes open.

He lifted his bound hands and twisted them to the side so he could study his watch, trying to read the hands in the dim light streaming in through the blinds. It was a bit after six in the morning.

Today is the day I'm going to die, Mike thought.

The thought brought him little comfort, but it also didn't bother him either. He felt like he'd truly died a week ago when the infant had exploded on him.

At least it will all be over.

Well, it'd be over for *him.* Reverend Victor would continue doing the same thing to the church until everyone in the town had been sent to heaven, Mike guessed. He felt a twinge of guilt at leaving his church behind with this monster, but tried to push it down.

I tried. I tried everything. *And they don't even want to be helped.*

Mike watched the sunrise through the blinds. The last sunrise he'd ever see. He wished he had a cup of coffee to go with it.

Eventually, Reverend Victor kicked open the door to the bedroom. He wore only underpants. His face wore a deep five o'clock shadow. In his hands, he clutched a suit Mike recognized as one from his closet.

"I went to your house and got you some more appropriate clothes. Gotta look good on your special day." Reverend Victor grinned. "Come on."

Mike pulled himself up and out of bed without question. He followed the reverend down the hall and to the bathroom.

Reverend Victor grabbed Mike's wrists and ripped off the surrounding tape. He repeated the process on his ankles, cringing at Mike's stench. Mike stayed silent, but gratefully stretched his sore limbs.

Reverend Victor gestured toward the bathroom. "Get that smell of death off ya. And get in these clean clothes. Get looking *exactly* like you would on any regular Sunday."

Mike didn't know why Reverend Victor wanted the details to be so perfect. The congregation wouldn't have cared if he'd marched Mike inside in his current state. The men would still thank him. The women would still fuck him. Nothing would change.

"Try *any* funny business—I'll stab you in the neck and dump your body in the closet after church," Reverend Victor growled. Mike cringed at the smell of onions and ketchup on his breath.

Reverend Victor pushed him into the bathroom. Mike pulled off his soiled suit. Being out of the garments felt even better than he'd expected. He stretched, basking in how it felt to be free of them. Reverend Victor's bathroom was small, with tile floors, a pink rug, a toilet, a sink, and a standing shower.

Mike kicked his clothes to the side and stepped into the shower, cranking the knob. The hot water hitting his skin felt incredible. He sighed, letting all the dried, caked-on blood slowly chip off of him and swirl down the drain.

He grabbed a bar of soap from the ledge and scrubbed it everywhere. Then rinsed. Then he scrubbed it again. And rinsed.

He repeated this process over and over, and he kept repeating it even long after the water had run clear. He wanted to stay in the shower forever, but he didn't want Reverend Victor to come barging into the room.

He cut the water and stepped out of the shower. His soiled clothes looked extra filthy now that his body was clean. He picked them up between his finger and thumb and dragged them over to the trash can. He let them drop.

Clunk.

Something solid hit the bottom of the trash can. Something much more solid than clothes.

Mike sucked in a breath. He remembered now.

He dropped to his knees and ripped his blazer out of the trash can, fumbling until his fingers found the inside pocket. He pulled out the steak knife he'd stashed in it a week ago.

Had he grown so depressed, so used to its familiar weight against his side, that he'd forgotten about it?

He swallowed, eying the dull blade. He still wasn't opposed to the idea of dying. But maybe he could kill himself now. Slit his wrists in the shower and make Reverend Victor have to drag him over to the church himself.

That'd get his stupid white suit dirty, Mike thought smugly. And then ...

I could kill him ...

BAM, BAM, BAM!

Mike jumped, and the knife slipped from his hands. He reached and snagged it from the air right before it clattered to the ground.

BAM, BAM, BAM! Reverend Victor pounded on the door. "Get a move on."

"Okay," Mike said, forcing his voice to remain even.

Hate coursed through his veins, stronger than blood. If Reverend Victor thought he was going to go down without a fight, he was sorely mistaken.

EIGHT

MIKE AND REVEREND VICTOR strode across the lawn between
the parsonage and the church. Wind jostled the trees, but with
the birds having long vacated the area, there was none of the
typical birdsong that Mike associated with Sunday mornings.

He walked with no restraints, his head held high. Reverend
Victor had drilled it into him that if he even *sensed* Mike was
preparing to make a break for it, he'd bust him over the head
with one of the hymnals.

Mike had nodded, keeping his head down. He tried to play
the part of the depressed, beaten-down man he'd been for the
past week. Reverend Victor couldn't know he'd found a teensy,
tiny sliver of hope. Or that his suit coat pocket now held that
hope.

Reverend Victor hopped up the steps to the church, grinning
as he opened the doors for Mike. He'd already fallen into his
charismatic persona, his face drawn into a bright smile.

Mike shuffled into the church. Before he could take two
steps, he felt Reverend Victor's firm hand on his shoulder. The
reverend steered him to the back pew, shoving him down hard
enough his butt smacked against the wooden seat painfully. The
reverend leaned down, hissing into Mike's ear.

"Stay here. Don't get up to piss; don't go get coffee. Make
small talk here until the sermon starts. When I tell you it's
your turn to go to heaven, you're going to hop up, cheer, and

celebrate like everyone expects. If you don't, I'm going to make your death ten times more painful."

The reverend's words spilled from his mouth and down the collar of Mike's shirt, rippling chills up his arms and back. Mike nodded slowly.

His heart hammered in his chest. He felt as if Reverend Victor could *sense* the knife in his pocket. But Reverend Victor just smiled, clapped Mike's shoulder, and walked away.

It didn't take long for people to trickle in. Doug stopped by and said hello to Mike, and they spent a few minutes talking about the fishing they were going to do this season if the Lord didn't call either of them up to heaven.

Mike wished Doug would go away. He wanted time to think. Time to plan.

Doug eventually tottered off to get a donut. And Mike, not wanting Reverend Victor to toss a hymnal at his skull, declined to follow along.

That left him alone to map out his next steps. He'd have to execute them carefully, and the more he thought, the more he realized he wasn't at all likely to kill Reverend Victor. Most likely, he'd fall flat on his face.

But he watched the reverend. He watched him shake the hands of a man whose wife he'd screwed the past week. He watched the man look at the reverend like he was some sort of god. None of them could see them for the greedy, trashy slob he was.

Well, Mike would try his damnedest to show them that Reverend Victor was no God. Let them worship the man when he had Mike's steak knife jutting from his neck.

Before long, the donut eating and casual conversation stopped. Every butt found its way into a pew, and Oakwood Baptist sang three hymns. Once the choir vacated the stage,

Reverend Victor slithered up behind the pulpit and began his incoherent babbling, earning thoughtful nods and teary-eyed "Amens!" from the congregation.

The clock hanging above Reverend Victor's office door ticked on and on as the Reverend told the church nonsensical facts. Mike felt himself growing more and more nervous with each passing second. His pits darkened with sweat. He bounced his foot and fiddled with the worn corners of the red hymnal in his lap.

In a matter of minutes, he was going to be sent to die. And all he had to stop it was a cheap steak knife. And on top of that—he was going to kill a man.

Would God forgive this murder? Would he find it justified? God approved when hardened murderers fried in the electric chair; was what Mike was doing any different?

Reverend Victor had killed no one directly—but he had knowingly given dozens upon dozens of people to that *thing* downstairs. How was that different from murder?

Mike prayed silently. He begged God for forgiveness. The sermon wound down, so Mike gave the Lord one last plea.

Lord, if I succeed and take this man's life—please let me see the actual gates of heaven. I think this is how you would want me to handle this trial you've given me. Please forgive me anyway, amen.

Reverend Victor leaned against the pulpit, smiling at the crowd. His brow was sweaty. He'd said a whole lot of nothing, but he'd said it forcefully.

"Oh, church, you folks are beautiful ... look how beautiful you are. I hate to part with any of your beautiful faces. But as you know, the Lord has given us something ..."

Here it was. The transition to talking about who would get sent to heaven this week.

"The Lord has laid a name on my heart, church. Someone who he wants to call home to do some amazing work in heaven, someone he doesn't want to suffer the horrors of death. Isn't that amazing, church? How we never have to face the Grim Reaper?"

"Amen!" several people shouted. The church nodded in agreement.

"No more heart attacks, strokes, automobile accidents, or any other worldly, painful deaths for your church. You get to go right up to the creator, don't you folks?"

The church responded with more forceful amens and a scattered round of clapping.

Mike's hands trembled uncontrollably. He grasped his knees, digging the fingernails into his flesh to steady his arms. He kept a neutral expression pasted on his face, but the putrid stench of the church dancing in his nose only egged his nervousness on.

The idea of going down and stepping in that damned closet made him want to jump up and scream. He didn't know how he was going to willingly enter the closet with it.

What even was it? He'd never found out. Was it a demon or an earthly monster? Maybe it was simply an animal.

Long, white fingers shaking the baby like it was dancing—teasing Mike.

He shuddered. It was not an animal, that was for sure. It was just something that crept down from the ceiling in the closet.

Mike focused back on Reverend Victor's sermon. "Ladies and gentlemen, I am proud to announce the Lord has called *Mike* home!"

Thunderous applause broke through the church. Everyone stood, turning to beam at Mike and clapping in his face. Mike sucked in a deep breath. His plan would only work if he acted exactly how Reverend Victor wanted him to.

He forced a huge grin on his face and stood, raising his arms like he'd won the lottery. People swarmed him, extending their hands in congratulations. Mike wiped his hands on his pant leg between each shake so people, hopefully, wouldn't feel how sweaty he was.

It was exhausting to celebrate and act like you'd just received the best news ever while you were simultaneously grappling with the possibility of your incoming death, but Mike tried his best. If he did it right, he could wipe that stupid, smug grin off Reverend Victor's face.

"Come on, everyone! Let's do this!" the reverend shouted. Everyone cheered and began filing toward the basement door. Mike got pushed to the front of the crowd.

The din and chatter of people behind him grew louder in his ears. The sweat in his pits doubled. His heart beat even faster. The closer he got to the basement, the less sure he was of himself. He felt as if he might collapse into a sobbing puddle as soon as they reached the bottom of the stairs.

You can't. Toby is dead. If you want to kill the man responsible, act naturally.

Mike kept his smile on his face. He trotted down the steps to the basement, even though his body begged him to turn back. He faced where the baby had exploded. Where he'd been forced to clean up the aftermath, and he kept a smiling face the entire time.

Alongside the horror and disgust, the familiar rage bubbled up inside him. Reverend Victor was forcing him to perform this charade all for *his* benefit. It was cruel. Sadistic.

Mike continued to shake hands and smile at people. They all blended into a gray mush. He didn't recognize who had just started coming to see the closet and who he'd known for 20 years. They were all the same to him now. All Reverend Victor's acolytes.

As the crowd funneled in, Mike found himself pushed farther and farther forward until he was right up against the closet door. He turned, unable to look at it head-on.

Is that thing in there now? Waiting for me?

Reverend Victor strode down the stairs last. His eyes zeroed in on Mike as he crossed the distance between them.

"You ready to go, Mike?" He grinned.

Mike smiled back, forcing himself to stand up straight. "Absolutely."

Reverend Victor grabbed Mike by the shoulder and turned to face the congregation.

"Well, church, this is where Mike tells us goodbye. Mike is one of the earliest members of Oakwood Baptist still at the church. It'll be so terribly sad to see him go, but we know the Lord has his reasons, doesn't he church?"

The church murmured their agreement. Reverend Victor's fingers dug into Mike's arm. He clearly thought that Mike was on the verge of fleeing.

Put me in your little closet. I've got a surprise for you.

Mike could feel the comfortable weight of the kitchen knife pressed against his side. How had he forgotten about it for an entire week? It was all he could feel now.

"Second Kings 2:11, And it came to pass, as they still went on, and talked, that, behold, there appeared a chariot of fire, and horses of fire, and parted them both asunder; and Elijah went up by a whirlwind into heaven." Reverend Victor turned down to Mike, his eyes alight with fake love. "Mike, thank you for everything. Please, enjoy heaven."

A stab of fear shot through him. *This is it.*

Reverend Victor opened the closet door. The stench doubled over, punching Mike in the gut and provoking a small gag, which he stifled as best he could.

The gaping jaw of the closet was dark—not even the swinging orange bulb was on. The tall shelves leered at him. The ceiling was dark. Panic built up in Mike's chest, swirling like a tornado, flushing his face red and sending his blood pressure sky-high.

For Toby. Do it for Toby, damn it.

Mike stepped through willingly even though his legs felt like jello and buckled all three steps, even though he wanted nothing more than to turn and run, even though he wanted to rip out his knife right then and jab it through Reverend Victor's smug little face.

He turned around, facing the congregation one last time. They watched him as one might watch a child walking into their first day of school.

They aren't going to like it when I kill him, Mike thought.

The last face Mike saw as the door swung shut was Reverend Victor's. The wrinkly, beady-eyed man gave him a final, wicked grin before clicking the door shut.

Mike took a shaky breath. He was alone in the closet now. But he knew that wasn't true... There was something in the ceiling waiting for him.

Did it come from the ceiling? Mike scanned the dark closet. The floor seemed intact, and there were no discernible trap doors. The walls were all covered with shelves, and minus the door Reverend Victor was standing in front of, there didn't seem to be any other entrances or exits. It had to be the ceiling.

BAM! BAM! BAM! BAM! BAM!

Reverend Victor pounded on the door, summoning the thing. Mike jumped. Any second, the fog would come. And then ...

Mike craned his neck and looked up. The ceiling was low, but he could tell the boards were loose. The creature would come from above. That conformed to what he'd seen with the child as well. The baby had dropped from the top. The hands had emerged from above.

Cheers from the other side of the door. He could hear the pop of the lights.

An involuntary whimper escaped Mike's lips. He had to be quick. He ripped the steak knife out of his coat pocket.

HISS!

Fog began pouring upon him. The sulfuric stench came with it, strangling him. He shoved his nose in his shirt, gasping breaths through his mouth. The stench bypassed these precautions with ease, laying thick on his tongue and cramming the smell of eggs, feces, rot, and wet dog deep into his nostrils. The smell brought back memories of a week ago.

He clenched his teeth and closed his eyes, shutting out the memories. He tried to imagine Reverend Victor standing on the other side of the door—both hands pressed firmly against the wood as he prayed. Mike only had one chance to get this right. He slid his hand up the door, trying to sense where the Reverend had placed his hand.

He could hear the muffled prayers coming through the door, but he couldn't pick out Reverend Victor's voice. If he could just locate the man's head, then he could—

The thing was near.

Wooden boards creaked above him, slowly sliding over each other. Fear shot through Mike's veins. The stench doubled over, rolling down over him thicker than the fog. He gagged, retching up bile. Reverend Victor commanded the church to pray louder to cover these sounds.

Mike felt the weight of a presence above him. Raw. Heavy. Pure evil.

He had to be quick. He ran his hands along the wall even as he heard—*felt*—the creature slipping lower and lower. The stench was unbearable. He was seconds away from puking. And he could hear noises. Sloppy, fleshy *noises.*

He picked a spot. It would have to be here.

God, if you give me anything, give me this.

Mike cocked back the steak knife and slammed it down as hard as he could, mustering up any and all strength he could pull from his body—hoping, *praying,* it could split the feeble wooden door.

SHUNK!

It did.

The knife buried itself to the hilt, sawing through the door with a dull scrape. All prayer, cheering, and singing stopped. Silence from the other side. Hopelessness crashed through Mike. He'd missed Reverend Victor's hand, and now the congregation was staring at the random blade that had appeared—

"AAAAAAAAARGHH!!!"

Reverend Victor bellowed in pain. Mike felt his knife jostle, heard the sloppy wet sounds of flesh extracting the metal from itself.

He'd hit Reverend Victor in the hand. Now he wouldn't be pressed against the door. Mike took a deep breath and launched himself up and into the door. He flung himself outward, into the foggy basement, just missing a spindly arm behind him swooshing and grabbing at the spot where he'd been crouched a second ago.

Nine

Reverend Victor stumbled backward, clutching his bleeding hand, face twisted into pure fury. Mike completed his jump out of the closet. By the flickering lights of the basement, he could see the knife dripped with blood. The Reverend's blood.

Mike and Reverend Victor locked eyes. Never in his life had he seen someone look at him with such pure hatred. His pupils burned with a black fire.

Reverend Victor opened his mouth—to bark orders, to call for help, Mike didn't know what. He didn't give a fuck. He had one goal, and he lunged for it.

He had no combat training and he wasn't a veteran, but he had a knife. And he had a chance.

He raised the weapon high over his shoulder, aiming for Reverend Victor's heart. The Reverend raised both hands, cowering under Mike's attack. And there, painted on his face, was fear. Fear of death. It brought Mike intense joy to see it on the man.

The congregation yelled out. Women screamed; men shouted.

He slashed down his arm. The knife hurtled toward the reverend's chest. It was dull. It was flimsy. It had just broken through a wooden door and was no doubt on its last legs. But Mike put enough power in his thrust to counteract all of those factors.

Doug's bodyweight crashed into Mike. The force diverted the knife's lethal trajectory to the heart. It tilted upwards—slicing through the top of Reverend Victor's ear.

Mike slammed against the ground—the impact redoubled the pain from all the wounds he'd earned in the previous weeks. The physical pain was nothing compared to the emotional despair filling his chest.

I didn't get him. I didn't get him—holy Jesus, goddamn! I didn't get him!!!

Doug ripped the knife out of Mike's hand, throwing it to the other side of the room so hard it clattered against the wall.

He yelled to be heard over the outraged roars of the congregation. "Why, Mike?? Goddamn it, why?!"

Mike wrenched his neck from Doug's grasp and looked up at the closet. The lights had stopped flickering, and he could perfectly see two long, white hands retracting back up into the closet.

"Look! Look up at the closet!" Mike screamed. No one heeded his demands. Several men had stepped over to Reverend Victor. They pressed their handkerchief up to his ear and hand. Mike heard one woman continuously screeching for someone to call an ambulance.

Mike wrenched with all of his might, trying to get out from under the portly man holding him down.

"You idiots! Look *look!* It's a monster—in the closet. He's killing us! He's killing us!" Mike roared. His screams fell upon deaf ears. Two more men came over to help Doug hold Mike down. A skinny, tall fellow kneeled on Mike's thrashing legs. A burly young guy held Mike's hands behind his back.

Reverend Victor stood. He had blood smeared on his face and a white-turned-red handkerchief wrapped tightly around his hand, but otherwise, he looked perfectly fine.

He faced the congregation, raising his fists in a victorious symbol. "Evil tries, but God tries harder!"

The congregation roared at this—hooting, hollering, cheering, clapping, jumping, praising, and crying tears of joy. The noise they made was deafening.

Mike screamed. "Look in the closet! Look up at the ceiling! There's a monster there who's been killing people. Toby the baby—I saw his body! I saw his lifeless body."

Reverend Victor scowled down at Mike. "Listen to the incoherent babbling of this heathen. It is no wonder God rejected him from heaven."

"What happened to him, Reverend?" Doug asked.

"Nothing happened to me, Doug! What happened to *you* people?!" Mike shouted. Doug bashed the back of Mike's head—sending his forehead colliding with the floor. Mike saw stars.

"Is he possessed?" a woman in the back hissed.

"Is he a Democrat?" one man gasped.

Reverend Victor stepped forward, looking down at Mike with an expression of pure hatred.

"I think he's just pure evil," Reverend Victor said.

The men holding him roughly pulled Mike to his feet. Mike sucked in a deep breath. "You all need to listen to me—he can't send people to heaven. There's something *in* that closet, something that's taking these people."

Doug smacked him across the face. "Blasphemer!"

Mike glared at Doug. Doug glared back. Mike looked at the congregation, searching desperately for a sympathetic face. Someone who might be on the fence. Someone who might hear him out.

He saw nothing but hatred in their faces. Their ears were closed.

The reverend's face was still alight with rage. He glared at Mike with pure anger, but there was also still a hint of fear in his eyes. Mike had no clue why—the reverend had clearly won.

Reverend Victor extended his hands, drawing a hush over the crowd. He stepped toward the middle.

"I have just received a message from God ..." he said.

The congregation gasped. Mike knew it wasn't the time, as his death was no doubt imminent, but he rolled his eyes.

"What'd he say?" Doug shouted.

Reverend Victor shot a look at Doug. A glimpse of annoyance crossed his usually jovial face. The mask slipped for a fraction of a second. Almost instantly, a big smile chased away the frustration.

"Doug, my brother, he told me something you folks are all gonna love to hear..."

A buzz filled the room. Wives and husbands looked at each other excitedly. Doug banged his cane on the ground eagerly. Mike eyed the stairs, but the men restraining him must've seen his head move because their fists gripped his arms even tighter.

"Ladies and gentlemen," Reverend Victor boomed, using his loudest, most authoritative voice. "God has sent us a sign ... and that sign was Mike. Mike was rejected from heaven for being pure *evil!* And that is a sign of things to come! The day of deliverance is here!"

Cheers, wails, moans, shouts, cries, and every noise in the vocabulary of a church-going Christian was spewed as Reverend Victor proclaimed this revelation from God. His eyes went wide. He waved his arms wildly.

"What does that *mean,* Reverend!?" Beth screeched.

Reverend Victor turned to her. "Beth. It means that tonight ... we're *all* going to heaven! Go home and finish your affairs because tonight, we're leaving this earth!"

No words could properly describe the pure emotion that filled the room after the reverend shared this announcement. But only a full 60 seconds after the words left his lips did it slow down. Beth was on the floor sobbing, and Doug had left a dent in the wood-paneled wall after a forceful bash of his cane. He now had his back pressed to it, sheepishly trying to hide it.

The congregation hugged each other. Men and women both sobbed tears of joy, shouting out praises to God and Reverend Victor.

Mike's mind raced. He felt like he was going insane as he watched the congregation celebrate their mass euthanasia.

"No! No, no, no!" he said.

The congregation paid him no mind, continuing to celebrate.

"YOU IDIOTS, HOW ARE ALL Y'ALL GONNA FIT IN THAT DAMN CLOSET!?"

Mike hadn't finished yelling before he saw Reverend Victor charging at him. The reverend cocked his fist, and Mike felt four gold rings mash into his skull. The room swam. He heard people cheer at the punch.

And then he felt another, but this one was from someone else. And then another from someone else. Then he felt Beth's feeble old woman's arm strike at his stomach. And then his head was alight with blows. Ringing filled his ear; pain ripped through him. And things slowly faded out.

Mike woke up confused. His body hurt, but it was nothing compared to the dull, pounding headache that filled his head. He groaned, but his voice sounded fuzzy. Distant. Was he in bed?

No. He knew he wasn't. But he did not know where he was.

He winced. The pain in his head pulsed—making any thought impossible. He clenched his teeth and bore down until the pain subsided. He gasped as it slowly released. It didn't go away. It just moved to the back of his head, thudding dully. He knew it was biding its time, waiting to return.

But why did his head hurt so damn bad?

He needed some ibuprofen. Hopefully, there would be some in the bathroom. There had to be a bathroom nearby.

He couldn't stand. His body remained rigid. For the first time, he felt spatially aware. He was sitting—sitting on a hard chair. His legs ached, and his butt was sore. He must've been sitting for a while. But why was he sitting? *Where* was he sitting?

He should open his eyes. That was a good idea.

He forced his eyelids apart. They cracked with sleep and dried blood. The room was fuzzy, lit dimly by an unfocused orb that Mike assumed to be a lamp. He blinked his eyes, willing them to see better. The fuzz sharpened a little, but not all the way. Everything still held a fuzzy outline, as if everything was coated in a thin layer of peach hair.

Mike looked around—and winced. Moving sent a crick jolting in his neck and brought the dull ache to his head full force. He kept moving his head, though, eager to see where he was and why he couldn't go to the bathroom to get a bottle of ibuprofen.

The tall desk and empty bookshelves of Reverend Victor's office came into view. He tilted his hands down and saw he was bound by duct tape to a metal folding chair.

Funny, he thought. And then the memories of everything came rushing back. He remembered the closet. He remembered stabbing the reverend. Then black.

A whimper came from behind him.

Mike whipped his head around, ignoring the nauseating ache it caused. There was a man in the office's corner. The man was also tied to a metal chair. He was bald and wore a mechanic jumpsuit. Along with his wrists and ankles, there was a thick strip of duct tape pressed against his mouth. The man looked familiar.

Mike opened his mouth. He didn't have any duct tape on his lips.

His pulse quickened. He began looking around the room again, this time for a way to escape. The window was the obvious option—it was dark outside already, how long had Mike been sitting here?—but how could he *get* to the window all tied up like this?

The door to the office swung open. Reverend Victor strode through. Pants-pissing fear roared through Mike.

The Reverend smiled. "Evening, Mike."

A thick brown bandage wrapped around his hand. A smaller white one was fixed to his ear.

"Like my bandages, Mike? I almost lost my life today!" He said it jovially, as if he were recounting a fun day at the park, but Mike could detect the vitriol hiding under the surface of his tone.

Something terrible is going to happen to me.

Reverend Victor sat behind his desk. The man in the corner of the room whimpered. His whimpering devolved into sobs. Big snotty snobs, hampered by the duct tape on his mouth.

"Who?" Mike slurred. It felt as if he had to re-learn how to use his mouth.

Reverend Victor scoffed. "Kirsty's husband. Came by my house last Tuesday drunk as a skunk givin' me some bullshit about "where's my wife and daughter waaa-waaa." You were asleep and taking up the guest bedroom, so I had to store him here."

"Let him ... go," Mike murmured. He felt like he was screaming, but his voice sounded very faint.

Reverend Victor rolled his eyes. "If I let him go, this suckers gonna run down the street yellin' that I took his family."

"You did."

"Yeah, but nobody needs to know that."

Mike scoffed. "They ... they love you. They wouldn't care."

Reverend Victor grinned. "Now you're getting it, Mike." He leaned forward. "I fucked her too. Buncha times."

Mike stared at Reverend Victor. The pastor continued, "But anyway ... just because I *can* do something doesn't mean it's smart. I could go out in the middle of Oakwood and stab somebody, and no one in the church would care. That doesn't mean I *should,* though."

Kirsty's husband continued to wail into his gag behind them.

"So you can't kill me," Mike said.

Reverend Victor tipped his head back and roared with laughter. "No, of course I can. The same way I can fuck any of these poorly educated fuck's wives. As long as I do it *privately.*"

"Do you have them hypnotized?" Mike snapped.

Reverend Victor laughed again like Mike was a petulant child who needed to be explained to. "You think *that's* the supernatural part? You think I need to hypnotize them to earn their devotion? That's what you don't understand about people, Mike. Humans, as a species, are *dying* to have somebody to unconditionally worship. Figures who can do no wrong and give us everything we want. You tell them what they like to hear, offer them something, and have an *ounce* of charisma, and they'll be in your pocket in no time."

Mike thought for a moment. "Then you're just gonna kill me," he spat. He was done with this nightmare that never seemed to end.

Reverend Victor sneered. "I told you I don't like doing that."

Kirsty's husband—Ted, Mike remembered now, his concussed brain offering the information—started flailing in his seat, screaming against the tape.

"Shut up, you big ugly cunt," Reverend Victor scowled.

"What are you going to do with me?" Mike said.

"Send you to heaven," Reverend Victor smiled.

Mike swallowed. "What's in the closet?"

Reverend Victor crossed his arms. He looked over at Mike as if he were appraising him. "You've caused me so much headache these past few weeks; I don't think I mind telling you. It's not like you'll be able to tell anyone." He leaned forward, his face darkening. "And I'd love it if you knew what's coming."

Reverend Victor stood. He paced to the window and stared out.

"I made a friend many years back, Mike. Well, it's not really a friendship, it's more of a business relationship. A very *fruitful* business relationship. See, we both had things we wanted but couldn't get. I wanted a nice car, nice clothes, women to fuck, money whenever I wanted it."

Reverend Victor turned to face Mike.

"My friend wanted human flesh to eat. But not just human flesh—human flesh consumed at the *height* of a person's joy. He says that the best a human tastes is when they've been ecstatic and then immediately filled with dread for around ten seconds. Something about the way a round of adrenaline mixes with dopamine—I don't fucking know, it grosses me out.

"My friend was having trouble achieving this balance. It was too tricky to find cheerful people to eat. Happy people are rarely alone in dark places. And though he can eat just plain scared—or hell, even apathetic people—nothing nourishes him like a joyful person turned scared."

Disgust twisted in Mike's gut.

"So, I make these people *very* happy, send them to him in the closet, and then he jolts 'em with a little fear and chows down," Reverend Victor said. "He also has ... a little *fun* with them, we'll say."

Mike's stomach roiled at the implication. But how could all this occur when the closet was always revealed to be empty?

"But ... we never see it in the closet?" Mike said.

Reverend Victor nodded. "He doesn't *live* in the closet. That's just the dumbwaiter. He lives in the walls. Has his meals there. I hear there's a particularly open spot between the floor of my office and the ceiling of the basement. But anyway, when I slam the door five times, that's enough to wake him up and grab his food."

"You can't get away with this," Mike said.

Reverend Victor's eyes lit up. "You think this is the first time we've done this? Mike, there are empty churches all along the country—the only thing left behind are rumors and whispers of a miraculous pastor with the ability to send people straight to heaven. Oakwood Baptist is not the first, and it won't be the last."

Mike's stomach churned. How many people had died to Reverend Victor and this ... *thing?*

"The police ..." Mike trailed off. A thick stab of pain bounced around his head, flushing out any ability to think.

"Who reports who to the police, Mike? Everyone's gone to heaven—willingly! No bodies to uncover, no unfinished business. What would they investigate?" Reverend Victor laughed.

"They wouldn't ... they can't just let that many people go ... it can't be that simple," Mike said.

Reverend Victor nodded. "Often, there's an especially curious dipshit—like you—who pokes their nose too far. But," he shrugged, "I always just send them to heaven too."

Reverend Victor sighed, growing sullen. "Of course, it can't last forever. Always gotta cut it short sooner rather than later. Have a big revival and wipe everybody out before the wrong person gets wise. It's a shame. I liked Oakwood Baptist a bit."

Mike shook his head, aghast. "Why do you do this?"

"Ahh, yes, back to what *I* want. Well, Mike, dozens of people disappearing means dozens of unaccompanied wallets. Dozens of bank accounts that can be drained before someone's divine ascension. Dozens of homes filled with expensive jewelry."

"You steal from them," Mike spat.

Reverend Victor waved his hand. "They sure don't need it anymore."

"You're sick," Mike said.

"And *you* are a dead man. That fucker, too," he jerked his thumb at Ted. "I hope you had fun being a complete asshole, Mike. You're gonna pay for it now."

Mike wanted to protest. To spit in Reverend Victor's face—but hopelessness was filling his chest. He just wanted it to be over.

"Do your worst," he mumbled.

Reverend Victor grinned. "Don't worry, Mike, I will. I just wish you'd be around to clean up the aftermath."

Reverend Victor strode across the room to Ted. He screamed and writhed as he got closer.

"Shut *up!*" He slapped him across the face. Ted's screams descended into sobs. The reverend grabbed his ear and yanked him to his feet. He produced a steak knife—*the* steak knife—from his pocket, then turned and flashed it at Mike. "Bet you wish you had this."

He sliced the tape at the man's ankles. Ted stepped his feet apart. Reverend Victor put the knife to his neck. "Make a move, and I'll shove this in your neck. Move."

Reverend Victor led him out of the office. His whimpers grew more distant, and Mike could hear them descending the steps into the basement. Mike realized they were alone in the church. Everyone else had gone home to prepare for their journeys to heaven. A few moments passed, and then Reverend Victor returned.

"Your turn, Mike. Not gonna try any more tricks, are you?" he said.

Mike shook his head.

Reverend Victor scoffed. "Don't give me any of that crap. You acted beaten down all week and then tried to kill me."

That won't be happening again.

Reverend Victor hacked through the duct tape binding Mike's ankles, then pulled him up. The whole world spun, and the pain in Mike's head tripled. His vision became even fuzzier. Reverend Victor forced him along, practically dragging him out of the office.

He shoved Mike through the darkened sanctuary, whistling, *Are You Washed In The Blood?* Reverend Victor opened the door to the basement and smiled at Mike.

"After you."

Mike shambled down the steps. He took them slowly, one at a time, but the world still felt as if it were spinning. His eyes made the steps look like one fuzzy gray blob.

Halfway down, he felt Reverend Victor's shoe on his back. Mike tipped forward, slamming into the stairs and tumbling down the rest of the way. He tasted fresh blood in his mouth from a new split on his already bruised and bleeding face. The pain barely registered.

Reverend Victor dragged him to his feet and steered him forward. Mike tried to blink, his vision sharper. The lights downstairs were on. He could see Ted—sitting in another folding chair, his back to the closet.

Reverend Victor dropped Mike in a folding chair about ten feet away from Ted. Mike faced him. Reverend Victor retied the duct tape around Mike's ankles—this time taping them around so he was bound to the chair.

Mike spat a glob of blood beside him.

It'll all be over soon. It's going to hurt like hell—but then it won't hurt anymore. It'll all be over.

Reverend Victor grinned at Mike. He'd won. He strode to the closet door and slammed his hands against it five times. Ted screamed against the duct tape on his mouth, eyes bulging, veins popping. Reverend Victor propped the door to the closet open.

"I want you to see *everything*, Mike," he said.

He strode to the stairs, leaving Ted thrashing and sobbing and Mike still bleeding from his face.

"Have a *helluva* time in heaven, you two!"

The door to the basement slammed above them.

HISS!

The fog began to fill the room.

TEN

TED THRASHED IN HIS chair, screaming against the duct tape over his mouth. The lights began strobing at a nauseating speed. Fog crept from the closet, covering Mike and Ted's feet in the clouds within seconds. Mike took a deep breath. He wanted to be calm when he died.

Ted didn't seem to share this opinion. He whipped his head back and forth hard enough that Mike worried he might snap his neck before the creature ever got to them. His stomach churned in pity for the man, but he knew there was nothing he could do. He couldn't even offer any words of comfort to him. He'd seen the aftermath of this creature. It doesn't look like they're in for a quick or painless death.

The stench came heavier, rolling out with the fog. Ted retched behind his duct tape. The stench hit him extra hard. This was his first time at the church, and he'd yet to be inoculated with it. Mike hoped he wouldn't throw up. He closed his eyes and forced his own stomach to quiet down. He breathed through his mouth.

Scrrrape.

Mike's eyes opened involuntarily at the noise from the closet. The lights flashed even faster. They illuminated two long, pale hands gripping the top of the door frame. Mike felt his face lose color. His hands trembled in front of him. He prayed one final time.

Please let it be quick. Please, please, please let it be quick.

The thing descended from the top of the closet—still obscured by the shadows, save for its hands. The closet light hadn't been turned on, so it remained shrouded in darkness as it lowered itself. Filthy, wet stench renewed in Mike's nose, ripping a gag from his throat.

Ted threw up that time. Puke shot out of his nose. Mike could see him gagging on the chunks stuck in his mouth by the duct tape.

A hand emerged from the closet, crouched low to the ground, feeling out against the carpet with bone-white fingers. *Long* fingers. Each one stretched out longer than a straw. They pawed at the carpet like an unsure dog.

More of the hand came, revealing a long, slender arm. It was extremely thin—thin enough you could slide it through the neck of a Coke bottle—but long. *So* very long.

Another arm followed the hand, testing the same ground its brother just did. Mike's heart hammered in his chest as he watched the strangely human shapes emerge.

Look away. You don't want to see it.

But he couldn't look away. It drew his eyes to it like a magnet. The lights flashed. Copious amounts of fog poured out around the arms, shrouding it and making it look like a cheap magic trick. The stench renewed in the air, pulling tears down Mike's face as if someone was cutting onions. Ted continued to scream, choking on his vomit.

It came out of the closet.

Long is the first word that came to Mike's horrified and concussed mind. Disturbingly, grotesquely, unnaturally, *long*. Everything about the creature was disgustingly skinny and disproportionately lengthened. It slunk out on all fours, spider-like fingers splayed on the carpet, knobby knees dragging behind it. The sight didn't look natural. It didn't appear as an animal walking how nature intended—it looked like a person walking on all fours to intentionally pervert nature's order.

Tight, white, paper-like skin wrapped around its body. Mike felt that if he touched the skin, it would surely crumble under his fingers.

The creature looked like a malnourished elephant. Gaunt and wasted even though it had been feasting on pounds and pounds of human flesh. An extended trunk dangled from its strangely human face. The trunk was leathery, hanging so low it dragged across the ground.

It looked up, and its piercing black eyes stabbed right through Mike's soul. Its trunk swung between the eyes like a pendulum.

"Oh God," Mike said.

Ted screamed again—even louder than all the times before. Mike could hear vocal cords snapping inside the man's acidic, vomit-laced throat. Poor Ted still couldn't see the creature, but Mike's face must've been enough to convey the gravity of the situation.

The trunk was not thick but, again, thin and emaciated, coated in a sticky green goo. The creature's mouth dripped the green fluid, too. Its jaw hung open, rows of green-flecked teeth filling a gaping, tongueless mouth. Deep, ragged breaths pulsed in and out of its maw. Mike could feel the stench emanating from the vile orifice. It filled his nose, attacking his smell receptors. He panted through his mouth. His stomach begged to release its contents.

And then, through the fog, Mike could see the thing's penis. The massive cock dangled from its elephantine body, dragging across the carpet like the trunk and cutting a path through the haze.

The lights continued to flash. The fog continued to pour. It had never come so much before. It now rose to Mike's waist and covered the freakish limbs of the creature—making it look like it was floating in a stormy sea.

A single piece of black fabric, perhaps once clothing, now filthy, ripped tatters, precariously hung from the creature's frame.

The creature grunted. It was the worst sound Mike had ever heard in his life. It boomed through the room—drawing more sobs from the poor man tied to the chair. The sound was not the unemotional grunt of an animal. It was the grunt of excitement. Of pleasure. It sounded like a man looking upon a naked woman.

It was a grunt of intelligent desire to do evil. This was no stupid animal feasting upon them only for nourishment. Mike knew in an instant that it would derive a psychological, and perhaps even sexual, pleasure from their death and dismemberment.

Ted screamed and thrashed, still unable to see the horrible thing behind him. He shook and rocked the chair so much it shifted closer to Mike an inch or two.

The creature crept up behind him, grunting and dripping green goo. Its trunk rose, snaking up the back of Ted's chair and running up and down the man's bald head, leaving a sticky trail. Ted froze. He went silent, trembling with wide eyes. They locked on Mike's, begging with him—*pleading* with him to do something.

The trunk slid down his arm with a rehearsed expertise. This was the first glimpse of the creature he got. His eyes opened so wide Mike thought his eyeballs might pop out of his skull. He thrashed with renewed vigor. But there's only so much you can do with your hands bound and your ankles fixed firmly to the chair you sit in.

The trunk left a path of wetness as it skirted down to his hand. It peeled off his wedding band, dropping it into the thick sea of fog with a small *tink*.

The trunk enveloped one of his fingers. Ted howled in pain, and Mike didn't understand why until the trunk slipped off of his finger and revealed the bleeding, pink, nail-less finger. The creature tosses the nail over its shoulder. It taps the wall and falls into the fog.

Ted bunched his hand in a fist—drops of blood dripping off it. This provided no obstacle to the creature. Its spindly hand appeared from the fog; long fingers pried Ted's hand open. Thin though it was, Mike could immediately tell the creature was *not* weak. It forced the mechanic's hands open with such force the man's fingers snapped backward.

Ted's eyes rolled back into his head. A guttural howl of pain escaped the tape.

The creature picked off each of the fingernails of his broken hand, tossing them aside as if they were peanut shells. The process went on forever. It took its time, savoring the pain inflicted upon the man with each pull. It didn't spare Ted's toenails, either.

Every time it ripped off a nail, and Ted let out a groan of pain, the creature would grunt—growing more and more excited as Ted's suffering increased.

Mike watched with horrified eyes as the massive dick dangling between the creature's legs stiffened. Blood rushed to the member, making the veins pop. It twitched every time one of Ted's nails hit the floor.

Once the man had been de-nailed, the creature slid its trunk up to his face. It removed the tape with a disturbing dexterity.

A stream of blood and vomit dribbled from Ted's mouth onto his lap. He sucked in a deep breath and let out a hoarse scream.

He didn't finish the scream before the trunk was in his mouth, probing inside him, making him splutter and cough—and then scream again. The trunk emerged, slithering from the mouth like a snake. It flicked something back. Something that landed on Mike's lap.

He looked down. By the flashing lights, he could see a bloody molar resting on his lap.

The creature continued to rip out Ted's teeth—tossing them to and fro as he screamed and bled from his mouth. The more pain Ted endured, the more excited the creature got. It grunted and snorted, bobbing up and down like an excited dog as blood poured over the man's chin like a faucet. Its veiny cock bounced up and down, smacking the floor with wet *plaps.*

The last tooth dropped to the ground. Ted cried silently, tears, blood, and vomit streaking down his face and into the fog.

The creature spun in a circle, hopping and grunting and finally sticking out its trunk straight in the air and letting out a triumphant—*HRRROOOOONK!*

The trumpet sprayed blood and green goop across the room in a fine mist.

It turned back to Ted and picked up his hand with its trunk, shoving the limb into its mouth and chomping down. Its dozens of teeth shattered the bones of Ted's fingers, tore through muscle, and severed skin. He ripped his hand back, clutching the bleeding, three-fingered stump close to his chest.

This has been happening in the walls of the church for months, Mike thought numbly. *They let this continue obliviously. I let this continue obliviously ... and knowingly.*

The creature spun around in circles—trunk and cock flapping loosely as it celebrated. Its cheers and grunts rattled the walls.

HRRROOOOONK!

The creature's excitement crescendoed. Its cock swelled with liquid, ready to burst. The creature leaped upon the chair that Ted was bound to, straddling the man like a stripper.

HRRROOOOONK!

It grabbed its cock in its white hands, masturbating the organ furiously. Then, in one fluid motion, it shoved it forward. The thick, bulbous tip pushed Ted's eyeball back into his skull with a horrible *sccclllllchhhh*. The man came back to his senses—bellowing in agony as the thing shoved its thick cock into the man's eye socket.

HRRROOOONK!

It bellowed. Then began thrusting. Ted's screams became erratic—then stopped altogether as the creature began thrusting faster, plunging its dick into the man's skull. Leathery testicles slapped against Ted's cheek. Mike watched its saggy ass as it pumped away. The man convulsed, writhing and shaking against his restraints.

And Mike thought that maybe, just maybe, he wasn't okay with dying anymore. Not like this. Not to this horrible creature.

It pumped away so fast that Ted's head started snapping back and forth. The man's jaw was lax. Mike hoped he had mercifully passed away. The creature reached a fever pitch, going at the man's head like a teenage boy at a pair of couch cushions.

HRRROOOONK!

White liquid exploded out of Ted's ears, nostrils, and the other eye hole. The monster's semen coasted over the gored body, mixing with blood and vomit and dripping into the fog.

The creature slipped off the chair, retracting its penis with a *pop* and leaving a gaping hole in Ted's skull. Cum and mushy pink stuff, which Mike assumed to be brains, cascaded out of the socket, down Ted's cheek, sliding down over his lips and into his mouth.

The creature lifted its hand to Ted's head, dragging its nail across his forehead and leaving a deep gash. It continued around his head, drawing blood. It peeled off the top of his scalp.

Ted convulsed again, shaking in the chair, toothless jaw chattering. Blood poured from the top of his head and filled the whites of his glassy eyes.

No ... no, I don't want to die. No, not at all.

The creature struck his head with a balled-up fist. The wet, gleaming bone cracked. A gasp escaped Ted's mouth.

Mike tugged at his restraints. His brain was swelling inside of his head from the repeated blows of the congregation, and things were hard to understand, but one thought was clear: no, he didn't want to die to this thing. He *couldn't*. He had to get out of here. He had to get out of here now.

He bent over, reaching his clasped hands into the dark fog. He fumbled around at his feet and the chair legs, trying to find the start of the duct tape. His eyes flickered up every few seconds, unable to look away from the vile thing mere feet away from him.

It beat at Ted's skull, sending chips flying and cracks spider webbing through the bone. Mike kept fumbling for the start of the duct tape. His fingers grazed alongside it—hope stabbed his chest. He grabbed it firmly and tugged. It barely gave. He was so weak...

Ted's skull cracked. The creature pulled off a big shard and tossed it behind him. The trunk slipped over his skull and inside. It pushed and prodded at his pulped brain, stirring it like it was a bowl of mashed potatoes.

Mike pulled, peeling the tape slowly but surely. His duct-taped hands made the task nearly impossible, but he persisted. His legs were the only thing fastening him to the chair. If he got those off ...

The creature grabbed a trunk full of mushed brains and shoved it into its oversized mouth. It gobbled it down—the sound of its mastication booming around the room. Mike worked faster—praying that the creature would stay busy with Ted longer.

He unwrapped and unwrapped and unwrapped. He could feel a sticky bundle of tape building at his feet. His legs slowly felt less and less restrained.

The creature's trunk was probing into the man's empty skull as if it were licking the plate clean. His body slumped forward, letting Mike get a perfect glimpse into the gaping emptiness of his skull. Then, the creature opened its mouth and unhinged its jaw like a snake. The gaping hole of its mouth became incomprehensibly large, expanding beyond the circumference of the creature itself. The skin of its cheeks stretched paper-thin, becoming translucent in the flashing lights.

And then it leaned forward, coaxing Ted's body into its maw. Its lips descended, slurping farther and farther until it had Ted from the belly button up in its mouth.

Crunch!

It snapped its teeth together and ripped its head back. Blood, guts, muscle, and sinew exploded as Ted's body ripped in half. The creature kicked back on its hind legs, cock, and trunk, flailing wildly as it chewed the top half of Ted's body.

Mike screamed, unwrapping the tape on his legs in a frenzy. He was so close.

The creature took four more big chews and then swallowed. The top half of Ted's corpse miraculously disappeared into the thing's skinny stomach.

Its enormous head turned as it plopped back on all fours. Its eyes raked over Mike like he was a hot meal. Mike bellowed again, pulling at the tape. His sweaty hands dropped it. The creature crept forward. Mike fumbled in the fog for the strand of tape. He couldn't find it. It was too thick to see.

The old, moldy, animalistic sulfur stench grew and grew—compounding with the fresh, coppery scent of blood and death. The creature grunted and bobbed its head, getting excited for Mike. Gore and green dripped from its chapped, wide lips. Its cock twitched, pre-cum beading at the head as it anticipated what the inside of Mike's skull might feel like.

Mike found the strand of tape. He yanked—pulling it around his ankles one last time. It gave, and his legs were free.

He leaped upright as the trunk hovered toward his fingers. Mike scampered behind the chair as if the pitiful metal could protect him from the creature.

It stalked forward—coming up to Mike's chest despite walking on its hands and knees.

But Mike had an advantage. He had the stairs to his back. If he could just make sure the creature wouldn't catch him, he could get out. The beast didn't *look* as if it possessed super speed, but it also didn't look like it was strong, and it sure as hell was.

It inched closer. It was now or never.

Mike grabbed the chair with his bound hands, lifting it high over his head. The creature lifted its trunk—Mike brought the chair slamming down. The metal crashed into the wiry frame of the creature, provoking an outraged *PPPPRRRROOOOOOOOWWW* from its snout.

Blood and green goop squirted around the creature as it disappeared into the fog. Mike didn't hesitate. He turned and sprinted to the stairs. He took them two at a time, hearing the furious grunts of the creature behind him. They grew louder. Mike knew it was in pursuit.

He burst through the door at the landing—charging into the sanctuary.

The baptistery on the stage boiled, water bubbled and sent steam up to the ceiling. The crucifix that hung above it had fallen—inverting and dipping the tip into the scalding water.

Mike didn't stop to observe these things. He kept running, sprinting through the row of pews and gunning straight for the exit. He twisted the knob and flung it open, leaping off the porch. The ground slammed into the bottom of his feet. The frantic pounding of his heart grew as he put himself farther and farther from the church.

He looked over his shoulder. Already, he was on the street. He expected to see the creature bounding after him, but it did not come.

He kept running until the church was as small in his vision as a dollhouse. But the creature did not come. Mike slowed, jogging a bit.

It hadn't left the building.

He remembered what Reverend Victor had said about doing things privately... this was not an evil that faced the outside world. It remained hidden—taking from the town and committing unspeakable acts, but all of it occurring under the veil of the good and righteous at the church.

Mike still ran. He turned and began sprinting down the street. His hands, still bound with tape, bobbed uncomfortably in front of him, the trees beside him turned to a dark blur, and his feet lost their feeling and became heavy bricks that were only there to slam into the pavement and briefly pick up before slamming right back down. His head throbbed and blinding white pain shot through his skull.

But he kept running. He kept running until he saw the faint, neon green and yellow glow of the 24-hour gas station on the outskirts of town. How long had he been running? He supposed it didn't really matter.

He'd survived. Reverend Victor hadn't been able to kill him. That elephant monster in the basement hadn't been able to either. The whole *goddamn* church was going to get themselves killed for that stupid beast's insatiable appetite.

But not him. Not Mike. He had tried to tell them the truth, and they hadn't listened. If they wanted to kill themselves over it—fine, but *he* wouldn't.

And the best part? They would think him dead. They'd assume the creature got him. The church would die. Reverend Victor would leave and take his monster with him. And Mike would be okay.

Mike stopped running once he reached town. He slowed to a walk. He probably looked strange to the people he passed—sweating in a dirty suit with a busted lip, two black eyes, and both hands duct-taped together. His legs burned, but everywhere else felt frigid. Without the heat of exertion, his sweat chilled, and felt miserable.

Time blurred a bit. He thought he remembered stepping into a restaurant, but when he blinked he was shuffling up the steps to his house. Oh well, he felt it would be better to be home. He collapsed as soon as he crossed the foyer. His legs spasmed and ached, but being off his feet felt so nice. He lay like that for who knows how long. A smile crossed his face.

He'd survived.

The smile immediately fell as he remembered Toby and the rest who *didn't* survive. Mike sat up, rubbing his head. Splitting pain ran through it. His whole body ached. He forced himself up and to the fridge and knocked back two cups of water with salt sprinkled in for his leg cramps.

After tonight, it would be over. Reverend Victor and the church would be gone.

Mike made it toward the shower but didn't make it. The exhaustion and his concussion caught up with him. He slumped to the couch.

I'll sit here for a few minutes to gather my thoughts.

He fell asleep before his head even hit the cushion.

Reverend Victor watched through the blinds as Mike streaked out of the church and tore off down the street. The man ran with remarkable strength for his age. How he'd gotten out, Reverend Victor didn't know. Sure, the duct tape could've been tighter—but the man had seemed so ready to die.

Reverend Victor sighed. He almost wanted to reward the man. Let him live. It was a pleasant change of pace from the babbling dumb-fucks he usually dealt with.

Rumors were fine. People who'd *heard* about a pastor who could send someone to heaven through a closet were no threat. But someone who'd seen it firsthand? Who wouldn't forget about it in a couple of months? That's how trouble starts.

He can deal with a few cops. But what would happen if a dozen came? No. As admirable as Mike's dedication to survival was, he would have to die with the rest of them.

Reverend Victor slunk through the dark, empty house. His frivolous purchases had all been packed in moving boxes. Tomorrow, he would rent a U-Haul and begin the drive to a little church in Tennessee that he knew was looking for a new pastor.

He picked up the phone and dialed.

ELEVEN

THUMP.

Mike opened his bleary eyes at the noise, again not comprehending where he was. It took him a few dizzy moments to grasp that he was on his couch.

Thump.

He jumped at the noise, whipping his head to face the front door. It had come from outside, but it hadn't been a knock, had it? No one would knock this late, especially not at his house.

His pulse quickened. He sat up a little straighter in his chair. Memories of what he'd just run from filled his swelling brain. But there was no way that Reverend Victor could have known...

BLAM BLAM BLAM!

Someone hammered on his front door. Mike squealed and leaped up from his chair.

BLAM BLAM BLAM!

A muffled voice came through. "Mike! It's Doug! Let me in!"

Mike clamped a hand to his mouth. Panic filled his chest. How did they know he was here? How did they know he was alive? How had they figured it out so quickly?

Mike crept backward, away from the door. His mind raced. He had to get to his car. He had to get to his car and get out of Oakwood for good. Get away from these *freaks.*

BLAM BLAM BLAM!

"Mike, we know you're in there. We just wanna ask you a question," Doug shouted.

We?! Mike thought in a panic. Who else waited out there? Mike continued to back away, stalking over to the stairs. Maybe if they came around back, he could jump from his bedroom window and get into the car before they had the chance to come back around.

Damn it, his *keys*. They taunted him from the rung right beside the front door. Mike groaned and changed course, stalking toward his keys.

"Mike, we've known each other for decades. Can't we just talk?" Doug yelled through the small frosted glass window beside the door. Beside the key ring.

Mike made a face. Mere hours ago, Doug had tackled Mike, slapped him, called him a blasphemer, and watched as he was beaten unconscious.

Mike crept forward, cringing at every creak of the floorboard. His heart hammered in his chest so hard he was sure Doug could hear the bump bump. He inched forward—arm outstretched to the key ring.

He could hear Doug murmuring on the other side of the door, talking to whoever else had come along.

Mike's hand was an inch away from the keys—

CRASH!

The frosted glass window exploded—a silver hammer forced through the frame. Shards of glass sprayed like confetti. Mike shrieked and snatched his keys off the ring. He turned and sprinted back toward the stairs as Doug's chunky arm probed inside and began fumbling with the locks on the front door.

Mike sprinted up the stairs. By the time he reached the top, the sound of the door slamming open roared through the house.

"GET HIM!" a man's voice boomed.

"KILL THE BLASPHEMER!" Doug yelled.

"HANG HIM FOR TREASON!" another yelled.

There are at least three of them, Mike thought deliriously. He threw himself into his bedroom and slammed the door. He twisted the feeble lock, almost wanting to laugh at how little protection it would provide him.

He turned to the window and threw it open. Two empty vehicles, a pickup truck and a van, idled on the street outside his house. The van's rear faced the house, and its trunk was open. Mike knew immediately that's where they intended to put him.

His heart clenched painfully as he heard thunderous foot-steps pounding up his stairs. It sounded as if an army was charging his little house.

There was no time to waste. He threw up the window. Icy air rippled over his skin. He peered down at the bushes and grass below him. Suddenly, the second story felt a lot higher.

BLAM! BLAM! BLAM!

The men pounded on the door. The puny wood rattled in its frame, ready to buckle under any pressure. Mike stuck his foot out and straddled the window frame. His stomach lurched.

Just drop. Just drop and get to the car.

He sucked in a deep breath. The door flew open. He turned his head and saw a charge of 5 men, led by Doug, pile into his room. He watched as they disappeared from his view, replaced by the sliding side of his house.

He'd pitched himself over without even thinking about it. The wind whistled in his ears and prickled at his face. His stomach lurched. Before he could even really comprehend he was falling, he—

Crunch.

As pain roared through his leg, he realized he probably should have at least *tried* to calibrate his landing a little better.

"Aaarghhhh!" he cried out, clutching his leg. He blinked away tears and looked down. His right leg twisted at a nauseating angle. Pain pulsed from it in blinding waves. He fell back on the grass, screaming in agony.

Through his bleary eyes, he could see the men stooped over the window, looking down at him.

"Back downstairs!" one of them yelled.

Mike groaned in pain and in fear. He had to get to his car and get *away*. He forced himself to roll onto his stomach, cringing against the wave of nausea and pain. The mob scurrying back down the stairs.

Mike forced himself to his knees. Any movement sent debilitating pain rocketing from his leg to his whole body. He clenched his fists—tears streaming down his face—and begged God for enough strength to just make it to the car.

Mike brought his left foot under him. Then he tried his right—

"AAAGHHHH!"

His vision went white at the pain. He smacked back into the grass, face first, sobbing and blubbering.

The booming footsteps of the men grew louder and louder until he felt their rough hands on him. He screamed himself hoarse as they hauled him up, paying no mind to his snapped leg.

"DON'T TAKE ME BACK THERE!" Mike roared.

"There are consequences to your actions," the man gripping Mike's right arm said.

"IF YOU ALL WANT TO KILL YOURSELVES FINE BUT DON'T TAKE ME WITH YOU!"

Doug kneed Mike in the crotch. "You've got a lot of nerve talking to us that way."

Doug smashed a strip of duct tape across Mike's mouth. Then he wrapped a thick bundle around Mike's wrists. Then they threw him in the back of the van, slamming the trunk and plunging him into darkness.

He moaned and clutched his leg, writhing and praying the pain would go away. The car lurched and gained speed as it rumbled down the road. Every bump in the road, every sharp turn, caused unimaginable pain as his body rolled onto his broken leg.

The physical pain was nothing compared to the turmoil in his chest as he sensed himself being taken closer and closer to the hellhole that was Oakwood Baptist Church. He thought of the thing in the closet. Ted's fingernails and teeth being removed before his eye-socket was raped. The baby being exploded against his Mike's chest.

The car ride felt as if it went on for an eternity. But eventually, he felt the car slow to a stop. He felt it jostle and shift as the men emerged.

Doug opened the trunk, letting icy air spill over Mike. He and the others grabbed Mike and dragged him roughly out of the trunk. Mike groaned and cried some more, his throat painful and hoarse from screaming. The men dragged him forward through the parking lot.

Mike struggled and thrashed through the pain as they dragged him closer and closer. The church building loomed over him, its cracked white walls menacing him in the moonlight. Wind whipped around the structure. Wood creaked.

The parking lot was full despite the lateness of the hour.

What is Reverend Victor going to do with all these cars? Mike thought before another stab of pain rendered his mind blank.

They dragged him into the building. Immediately, his ears filled with the dull din of hurried conversations coming from the open basement door. The men holding him marched him toward it. The trip down the stairs was the worst yet because Mike *had* to put weight on his broken leg every other step. He wanted to drop and flop down the stairs, but with Doug directly in front of him and a few men behind him, it was impossible. When he reached the bottom, he started weeping again.

The basement bustled with excitement. Everyone had taken the brief trip home as an opportunity to change into their finest clothes. The men all wore suits in various states of ill-fitting. The woman had adorned their most floral and bright dresses, putting on as much jewelry as possible for good measure.

People rush around the room, chattering and shouting and hugging and cheering and celebrating. Mike saw Reverend Victor at the back of the room by the closet. He stood by a folding table. Upon the folding table was a large wicker basket. Already half full of cash, watches, wallets, and purses, Mike watched as a woman came over and emptied her purse into it. Cash, hard candies, lip balm, and a bracelet fluttered down. Reverend Victor said something to her. She shrugged and tossed in her purse after the items.

Mike's stomach churned. How could they not see it for what it was? How could they not see that Reverend Victor was bleeding them blind?

Of course they wouldn't see it that way. No, Reverend Victor was just being polite and giving them somewhere dignified to place their earthly possessions before their ascent to heaven.

The basement was hot. Filled with the sticky sweat and odor of anticipation. Eventually, people noticed him. Drawn out of their eager fervor, they scowled at the sight of him.

"Why is the blasphemer here?" a short, stout woman cried.

More heads turned. Men and women, young and old, all regarded him as you might look at an ant swimming in your soda. A bulb had gone out in the lights overhead, making the room dimmer than usual. The harsh, whitish-yellow light beaming from above made their faces look sallow and gaunt.

None of them paid any attention to the fact that his leg jutted out at an odd angle. Or that he was duct-taped to hell. Or that he had been a member of their church for 20 years, and they were treating him like a criminal.

"Ahh yes ... the *evil* is here," Reverend Victor said. He strode up through the crowd with a solemn face. He had dressed up for the occasion, wearing his nicest white suit and pristine brown loafers. A chunky gold ring shined from each one of his fingers. A watch ticked on each of his wrists.

All their money can't buy him tact, Mike thought bitterly, scowling at the reverend's gaudy fashion.

The congregation heckled him, throwing jeers and insults.

"Traitor!"

"Treason!"

"Blasphemer!"

"Anti-Christian!"

With all the abuse he'd endured, both physical and mental, Mike didn't expect the jeers to hurt so badly. But they did.

Reverend Victor shook his head slowly, placing his arms behind his back and pacing in front of Mike.

"Now, as you all know ... the Lord almighty rejected Mike from heaven. And we wondered why. Why would God reject our beautiful Mike." Reverend Victor turned to Mike, running a ring-clad hand across his cheek. "Our Mike, who was so upstanding and faithful. Well, folks, that Mike is a lie."

Gasps from the congregation.

"He's not a traitor—he was never one of us to begin with!"

"Lord, no!" an old lady squealed.

"Mike was an evil—hidden and waiting to pounce. Beneath that meek little face is a stone-cold killer. A monster! A *predator!*" Reverend Victor waved his arms wildly as he spoke. The congregation gasped and shook their heads and clapped their hands to their mouths and whispered to their neighbors that they just couldn't believe *Mike,* of all people, was evil.

Mike hung his head. He had no voice to defend his name. Even if he did, no one would listen. Not if Reverend Victor was telling them otherwise.

Reverend Victor kept his solemn face, but his eyes came alive. The two little black dots danced greedily over the congregation, soaking in their shocked faces. Even if he did all of this for monetary gain, Mike could tell the reverend enjoyed whipping the crowd up into a frenzy.

"Mike was horrible, folks, and we were *blind* to it. He is, without a doubt, the *worst* member of this church's history. It's no wonder God rejected him... he embezzled offering money."

Gasps from the congregation.

"He got high on every drug known to man!" Reverend Victor roared, waving his arms as if he were imitating the boogeyman.

The congregation squealed. Women jumped up and down in rage. Men clenched their jaws and balled their fists.

Reverend Victor dropped his shoulders, leaning low and speaking softly.

"He raped *children.*"

An indignant cry rose from Mike's throat, and he thrashed against the hands that held him once more. He couldn't take *that* accusation.

But then there was a knee in his gut. The impact expelled all the air from his lungs. And then a fist collided with the back of his head. And then someone gave a sharp kick to his broken leg, and the world went white again. His ears filled with a shrill *eeeeeeee.*

When things came back, Reverend Victor was calming the crowd down. They looked ready to tear Mike apart, limb from limb.

"Now, now, church! Don't let this dangerous criminal ruin our joyous evening. This is an evening of celebration—for we are going to *heaven!*" Reverend Victor shouted.

Thunderous applause rang through the basement. Reverend Victor turned to face Mike again. He grinned. "However. It seems only fitting that before we go to heaven, we should send Mike to hell."

Cheers, hooting, and hollering filled Mike's ears—mixing thickly with the dread in his chest.

Doug grinned and bounced on his feet. "Do you have another closet for that, reverend?"

A flash of annoyance crossed Reverend Victor's face as he regarded Doug, but he quickly pasted it over with an eager grin.

"No ... we'll do this one the old-fashioned way. Let's kill him!" Reverend Victor said.

Cheers erupted among the congregation. Doug pumped his fist and shouted, "Let's hang him!"

Reverend Victor looked down at Mike, a triumphant smirk painted on his face. The two men locked eyes, and Reverend Victor spoke, but only Mike heard.

"I think we can do better than that."

TWELVE

THE MEN DRAGGED MIKE over to the table with the basket of money. Doug and another fellow held him as the congregation bustled about, chattering about how they were gonna kill Mike. Judging by the little snippets he heard, the popular sentiment seemed to be hanging.

Mike's mind raced as he tried to think of a way out of this. No solutions came to mind. Dozens of people, an evil pastor, and a hellish monster were all intent on seeing him dead. His odds were less than ideal. Panic swelled like a balloon in his chest and seemed to exacerbate the pulsing pain in his broken leg.

His eyes darted across the room, searching for a weapon, an exit, or an answer. They only found gleeful faces intent on killing him. Mouths moved to call for his hanging. People made rude gestures toward him. A few of the men seemed to itch to get up front and get a punch in on him before he was killed.

Mike tried to force himself to think of a solution, but his head was hurting so damn badly. Pressure was building and building between his ears, feeling like it would pop at any moment.

Reverend Victor slinked over and pulled Doug aside. He whispered in the man's ear. Mike's stomach churned as he saw a look of pure joy spread across Doug's face. He looked like a kid who'd just been told they were going to Disneyland.

Doug grabbed another man and they both jogged up-stairs. Reverend Victor smiled and stalked over to Mike, standing nose-to-nose with him.

"Sorry, Mike," he said, not looking sorry at all.

He turned back to the closet. Mike's heart leaped as he expected Reverend Victor to summon the horrible crea-ture. But the reverend just opened the door and turned on the light. He rummaged around through the boxes, then emerged. He held several hammers and two boxes of ex-tra-large nails.

Doug and the man returned down the stairs, carrying the crucifix that hung above the Baptistry.

It felt as if all the blood in Mike's body had drained out of his feet and onto the floor. His legs trembled uncontrollably. He wet his pants.

Reverend Victor cackled. Mike screamed against the duct tape on his mouth. He slammed his hands against his non-broken leg, trying to break the duct tape.

The congregation cheered in celebration at the appear-ance of the cross. They cheered even louder when they saw Reverend Victor holding hammers and nails.

Mike reached up with his bound hands and ripped the duct tape off his mouth.

"STOP NO! NO, YOU CAN'T MEAN IT!" Mike yelled. His voice came out high, a pitiful screech. Two men swarmed him and smacked the duct tape back on his mouth. One of them kneed his broken leg again. Mike squealed.

Reverend Victor grinned. "Rough him up, boys. Don't be too nice."

Mike thrashed like a wounded dog against the hands that gripped him. Doug and the other man were lowering the cross at the other end of the room. It seemed massive now that it was off the wall. The wood landed on the carpet with a thud. Then, all eyes turned to Mike.

He bucked and thrashed and kicked and screamed and flailed and cried and choked. He freed his right arm from his captor and launched a flailing punch. It connected, socking the nose of the man. He made an "oomph!" sound and clutched his face.

Before Mike could get any further, Reverend Victor stomped on his broken leg. The already snapped bone crunched even further. Mike screamed so hard the hastily reapplied tape burst off his mouth. His leg collapsed further inward, now sitting at a sideways 90-degree angle. Bone jutted from his knee. Blood dripped onto the carpet.

The congregation cheered, whooping and hollering at the pain Reverend Victor had inflicted on him.

"Who wants to send this bastard to hell!?" Reverend Victor shouted.

Deafening applause filled Mike's ears. His stomach roiled with nausea. He could feel his skin wet with sweat. His head grew fuzzy. Things seemed to become grayer than they should be. The rough hands on him dragged him forward.

A path cleared. On either side of him was a crowd of the people he'd lived in this town with for 20 years. The people who he'd gone to church with for two decades. Their faces showed nothing but pure glee as he screamed and howled. They smiled and danced as his bloody, gored leg dragged along the carpet and left a trail of hot blood.

The arms brought him to the crucifix. He wanted to fight back—to get up the stairs and get away. But he was too weak. They were too strong. His head swam, close to passing out as it was.

They flipped him around and pushed him down. He landed on the cross—his spine crunching against the hardwood. He groaned and tried to sit up. A dozen hands shoved him back. The congregation converged together, holding him down. They ripped the duct tape off his hands and stretched his arms out to the arms of the cross.

"AAAAARGGHHH!"

A short old lady with gray hair—who had always given Mike a hard candy on Sunday mornings—was now jerking at his broken leg as if it were a child's cowlick, trying to get it to lie flat on the cross. Mike blubbered, screamed, and flopped like a fish until—

SNAP!

All feeling left his leg. Numbness spread down his right side. He suddenly got even more sweaty, and he knew it would do him no good to look and see what had happened to his leg.

Reverend Victor came strolling up. The crowd parted for him. He smiled down at Mike, his beady little eyes alight with glee. Mike knew exactly what the man was thinking.

I got away with it, Mike. I got away with it before, I got away with it now, and I'll get away with it however many times I want. Until I get sick of all my money or a heart attack strikes me dead, I'll keep getting away with it.

Mike was a fool to stand up to him. He knew that. But it was too late now.

"What are you waiting for? Have at it!" Reverend Victor said. He passed out the hammers and nails to greedy hands. Every pair of foggy eyes showed an eagerness to drive a nail through Mike's flesh.

His heart hammered so hard he thought it would burst. He felt like a patient underneath an operating table, with a few dozen surgeons dressed in their Sunday best staring down at him. They ran wide eyes over him, licking their lips in anticipation, sweaty hands gripped around the wooden hammer handles.

The scent of wood filled Mike's nose. He figured that was the scent Jesus smelled at his crucifixion 2,000 years ago.

The first nail went into his arm.

Mike shrieked until his vocal cords ripped and bled. But the pain in his throat was nothing compared to the searing, pulsing agony shooting from his arm like electrical shocks. He tried to recoil and bring his arm to his chest and nurse the wound—but his arm didn't budge, driven to the wooden crucifix with the nail. Blood spurted around the nail head, deeply embedded in his skin.

The pain doubled as another nail followed its brother. This time, Mike could hear the individual strikes of the hammer as it drove the freezing metal into the warm flesh of his arm, pounding through tissue, veins, muscle, skin, and wood.

Even with the pain exploding in his right arm, he could feel the gentle press of the next nail balancing on his left arm.

BAM!

The hammer sent it down. Blood sprayed from his wrist, and the pain mirrored to his left arm.

BAM! Crunch.

Mike felt this nail explode through the bone, sending the shards exploding inside of him. Warmth cascaded over his arm as the blood poured out of him.

The people below joined in the fun. Though he no longer felt anything in his right leg, he felt acutely—as if his body were making him experience sensations in his left leg twice as hard to make up for it—as the nails were driven into his foot. Sharp, burning pain radiated up his legs and through his whole body as the metal invaded him and bound him to the cross.

The congregation did not treat this as a biblically accurate crucifixion. This was no children's drawing. There wasn't a nail in each palm and one for the feet. The congregation hammered nail after nail after nail into his flesh. His arms glowed silver in the dim light as dozens of nail heads gleamed from his flesh. But the congregation kept pounding, hammering a nail into any open space on his limbs.

Time lost its meaning, and the only thing that became real was the feeling of metal intertwining with flesh. The feeling of blood flowing freely from his body and coating his arms. The smell of copper, nails, and wood in his nose.

The faces above him turned hazy. The lights seemed to grow dimmer. The pounding of the hammers and excited chatter of voices dulled. Mike lay like that for a while. Then the voices became clearer ...

"3 ... 2 ... 1 ..."

Motion lurched him forward. The congregation lifted the cross. Gravity yanked at his body, pulling him forward, but the nails held strong. His body squelched as the dozens of wounds shifted around the metal. His body lurched forward, pulling his shoulders from their sockets with a wet *pop*. Searing pain blossomed in his chest and arms.

The congregation propped the cross against the back wall. It felt precariously placed, as if it could pitch over to either side at any minute.

His eyes rolled. A long groan escaped his lips—but he felt like he couldn't get all the air out of his lungs. He spluttered and tried to exhale, shifting on the cross. Every movement tore more of his flesh on the nails. Every movement sent bone grinding along the metal.

He flickered his eyes down at the congregation. They stared up at him with smiles on their faces and blood on their hands.

"Now, who wants to go to heaven?" Reverend Victor said.

Excited cheers. Mike opened his mouth. His dry lip split. A ragged breath spat from his chest.

The congregation flocked around Reverend Victor, thanking him and praying upon him. He kept a careful distance from anyone with Mike's blood on them.

"Will you go to heaven with us?" a woman asked.

Reverend Victor nodded. "Of course. We're all gonna walk to those golden gates, and I'm gonna be right there with you."

Drip, drip, drip, drip, drip. A puddle of Mike's blood formed under him. He felt so lightheaded.

"Well, church, this is it. Let's go," Reverend Victor said. He turned to the closet door and slammed his hands against the door five times.

BAM! BAM! BAM! BAM! BAM!

Each slam reverberated through the building and rattled Mike's cross, sending tiny vibrations of pain through each nail wound.

HISSSSS!

The lights flickered and fog filled the room. The congregation cheered and celebrated. Many fell to their knees and prayed. Couples kissed and embraced. Men jumped in the air and pumped their fists. Women succumbed to tears.

A sick smile spread across Mike's face as he realized the congregation would finally have to reckon with the truth.

The door to the closet slammed open. The creature emerged in a stench-filled, fog-drenched cloud. It was still long and abnormal. Walking on all fours with a wrinkly foreskin trunk dragging along the carpet. Its cock was already hard and oozing. It bucked and danced, eager for the feast Reverend Victor presented it with.

The congregation did not flinch at the horror. They did not cower from the demon that faced them.

"I'M READY TO GO TO HEAVEN!" Doug shouted, running up and falling to his knees in front of the creature. Doug's clothes were gone in a flash, ripped off by the creature's spindly fingers. It ripped off his nails with a systematic practice, then moved to his teeth next. Doug howled in pain as blood dribbled from his hands and mouth. But he praised God and Reverend Victor through the entire process.

"Thank you, Reverend Victor!" Doug called out before the thing rammed its dick into the man's toothless mouth. Doug spluttered and gagged as the creature fucked his throat. While it grunted and moaned, it ripped off Doug's scalp, cracking away at his skull like he was an egg. Doug squirmed and writhed, blabbering unintelligible praises for Reverend Victor and God around the cock of the creature.

The congregation cheered and thanked God and Reverend Victor for taking them to heaven as the creature orgasmed, pumping thick, white semen into Doug's head. It exploded out of his nostrils, eyes, ears, mouth, and the hole in his skull. The creature's trunk slithered over his body, probing into Doug's skull and shoveling his cum covered brains into its mouth. No one ran or cowered from the blood-covered thing as it threw Doug to the ground and began eating his legs.

They cheered as the creature worked its way up to the man's groin, slurping and slobbering as bone and flesh worked their way down its throat. It reached Doug's groin, ripping off his penis and tossing it behind it into the fog.

After he'd worked his way up to Doug's stomach, he discarded the rest of the man's corpse, eager to have someone else.

It came for a woman next, tearing off her nails and ripping out her teeth before sucking out her eyeballs and fucking the spot they'd once rested in.

The congregation cheered and thanked God and Reverend Victor for this miracle.

Reverend Victor sat at the table, rifling through the basket. He had gathered all the cash out of the purses and wallets, building up a thick stack in his hand. He paid no attention to the congregation's slaughter or the thanks they gave him with their dying breaths.

The creature made his way through the congregation. The air was thick with death. The floor was a pool of blood, teeth, and fingernails. Bodies lay face up, face down, and sideways. Whoever remained praised Reverend Victor and God while the thing fucked every hole they had and slurped up their bodies.

Reverend Victor stood up, a thick wad of cash in his hand, and stretched. He crept across the basement, careful to avoid a drop of blood getting on his shoes, and stopped in front of Mike. He stopped, looked up at the man, and smiled.

Reverend Victor reached out a single finger and pushed on Mike's side. He barely felt the pressure, but it was enough. The cross scraped along the wall and began its descent. Reverend Victor scurried up the stairs.

The cross hitting the ground ripped Mike from all 67 nails that had impaled him. He landed on his gut, gasping for air, his body filling with blood where there shouldn't be blood.

He lay among the rest of the dead, watching as the thing prowled toward the last standing member of the congregation.

Beth, wearing a hideous yellow dress, stood among the blood and broken bodies of her church. Her pastor had just run out the door with all of their money. She looked at the demonic monster that stood before her. Its cock twitched, still dripping with blood and semen.

"Thank you, God, for sending Reverend Victor to us!" she squealed.

The creature ripped out her teeth and tore off her fingernails. It punched a hole in her gut and fucked the wound, cumming directly in her torn stomach before burying its face in her midsection and devouring her insides. It cracked her skull and devoured her brains.

ACKNOWLEDGEMENTS

Many people helped make this book possible, and I'll try to thank as many of them as I can.

First, thanks to my editor, who never grows impatient with correcting my terrible use of commas.

Thank you to all of my family: my wife, Ruby, for reading my vile creations; my sisters, Stella and Beatrice, who are supportive of all my endeavors; and, of course, my mother and father, who I don't think intended to raise me this way, but support me all the same.

Thank you to Jesy Boales, who offered critical feedback on a very early draft of this story and helped shape it into what it is today. And thank you to all of my beta readers, who took the time to read a messy draft of this story and offer their thoughts—I honestly have no idea what I would do without you guys. Seriously. Thank you to V.S. Lawrence for all the amazing advice and support, and to everyone else on Instagram who has been so kind and welcoming of me to the indie horror community.

Thank you to the amazing people at r/extremehorrorlit, who've supplied me with tons of incredible recommendations over the years, and who were kind enough to be ARC readers for this book.

Thank you to Clive Barker for all of the amazing, fucked-up stuff you wrote, and for being kind enough to shake my hand when I was starstruck in your presence.

And finally, thank you, reader, for reading! I hope you enjoyed it, and if you did, I'd love for you to leave a review on Amazon, Goodreads, or scrawled in Sharpie on a bathroom stall.

ABOUT THE AUTHOR

Nicholas Gordon is a horror author who has been trapped in the Nightmare Realm since 1954. Known for his outlandish concepts, he often visits the dreams of others to find inspiration for his stories. He has written horror fiction such as *Hallowed Be Thy Gore, Lorenzo Lion's Pasta Arcade,* and *Doctor Wegman's Miracle Mist.* He has somehow acquired a cellphone, and you can find updates on his latest projects on Instagram @nicholasgordonwrites

Printed in Great Britain
by Amazon

60871308R00091